Henry Stewart Cunningham

Lord Bowen, a Biographical Sketch

Henry Stewart Cunningham

Lord Bowen, a Biographical Sketch

ISBN/EAN: 9783743346376

Manufactured in Europe, USA, Canada, Australia, Japa

Cover: Foto ©Raphael Reischuk / pixelio.de

Manufactured and distributed by brebook publishing software (www.brebook.com)

Henry Stewart Cunningham

Lord Bowen, a Biographical Sketch

LORD BOWEN

A BIOGRAPHICAL SKETCH

BY SIR HENRY STEWART CUNNINGHAM
K.C.I.E.

PRINTED FOR PRIVATE CIRCULATION
1896

PREFACE.

I HAVE to acknowledge my obligation to several of Lord Bowen's friends who have helped me in the compilation of this sketch —notably, to the Hon. George Brodrick, Sir Mountstuart Elphinstone Grant-Duff, Lord Justice Fry, Lord Davey, Mr. Justice Mathew, Mr. Bullock Hall, the Dean of Westminster, Professor Robinson Ellis, the Rev. E. Cole, and the Rev. A. Austen Leigh, who have been good enough to furnish personal recollections or letters.

These communications, too long to be conveniently embodied in the sketch, and too valuable to be curtailed, are collected in a separate volume; but I have taken advantage of the writer's permission to make free use of them whenever it seemed desirable for the purposes of the memoir. As I am writing for Charles Bowen's family, I have not attempted to delineate phases of domestic life with which they are far better acquainted than I, and of which they will, probably, prefer to treasure the recollection undisturbed by any record coming from without the home-circle. On the same ground, I have sometimes inserted letters which, from their familiarity, might seem scarcely fitted, as they were certainly not intended, for the eyes of any but intimate friends.

H. S. C.

November 12, 1895.

LORD BOWEN.

WHEN a friend, loved and admired, passes away from us, there is a natural desire for something which may serve to give distinctness and permanence to the impression which he made upon us in his lifetime. Such a desire is reasonable. When nothing of the sort is done, we become more than ever conscious of a loss which, in one sense, grows with the lapse of time. The definite outline becomes blurred; year by year the figure stands out in less bold and clear relief; the colours fade; recollections, however affectionately cherished, become vague, faint, and inaccurate. So the dull processes of oblivion

B

begin.   Natural, however, as such a wish may
be, its fulfilment presents grave difficulties to
him who attempts it.   It is no easy task to
delineate or analyze the qualities which have
combined to form an impressive and delightful personality.   So much, in such cases, is
indescribable, or describable only by reference
to those inner and subtle phases of character
which cannot be dragged into publicity.   We
know by melancholy experience how perilous
is the attempt to portray, through the cold
medium of written description, the influence
of personal charm.   The pen, however, con-
scientiously handled—is, as a hundred ambitious
failures remind us—but a coarse and feeble
instrument for the appreciation of the name-
less magic, the infection of intellectual or
spiritual mood, the moral magnetism, the
indefinable influence on heart and nerve, which
give some favoured natures so powerful a hold
upon the affections of their fellow-men.   The
volatile essence escapes while we examine it.

The residuum is always disappointing. How vapid, trivial, and overstrained seems often the recorded eloquence which, we know, stirred great assemblies to the quick, "shook the arsenal, and fulmined over Greece"! How commonplace the treasured sayings of historical conversationalists! What less exhilarating than the array of witticisms with which too faithful chroniclers justify the reputation of accomplished members of Society! Whence, we wonder, came the magic which gave phrases such as these their potency over the hearts and intellects of mankind? As well ask whence comes the magic of music, or the charm of the landscape which fades from our view before we have drunk our fill of its delight.

The difficulty of adequate portraiture is enhanced in the case of men whose energies have been concentred on an absorbing profession. Such a man's real work, the serious efforts and successes of his career, his intellectual idiosyncrasies, his moral gifts, are known to a comparatively narrow circle of observers, who watch him from day to day at his task, and are competent to form a just estimate of his achievements. The outside world must take him largely on trust. It sees the result in his successes, his rise to eminent position, his selection for important and difficult duties, the professional ascendency which the verdict of his contemporaries accords. But the real nature of these successes it knows only by hearsay. The distinguished judge leaves no adequate monument but his judgments; and these are accessible and intelligible to none but the few who possess the requisite knowledge, skill, and assiduity to study them understandingly. Outside his Court and the Reports in which his utterances are recorded, he is—so far as any real appreciation of his powers goes —almost unknown. If he lapses into literature, or amuses himself with Society, it is in leisure moments when his real business is, perforce, at a standstill; when an exhausted brain or shattered bodily powers warn him from continued intellectual strain; when his doctor has insisted on an interval of idleness, and bade him, if he wishes to escape from an impending collapse, to devote himself strenuously to being amused. The world, accordingly, never sees him at his best—never knows the real man, in the full vigour of body and mind, in the full swing of unimpaired energies, the delightful consciousness of intellectual prowess. When he writes, it is probably for the purpose of diverting his thoughts from topics whose too engrossing interest has overtaxed nerve and brain, or, as a *tour de force*, in some rare moment of leisure snatched from the turmoil of a professional career. When he shines in drawing-rooms, it is often because he feels incapable of shining with his proper lustre in Court. He is trifling because Nature has rebelled against too protracted seriousness. The bow is unstrung that it may recover its elasticity. Such men's relaxation is likely to be more edifying than the strenuous activity of less-gifted natures; and Society, dazzled and delighted, forgets that the performance which it admires is not the measure of what the man can do, but the pastime with which he has been ordered to refresh himself as the penalty of overtaxed energies and the condition of possible return to the serious business of existence.

But there are graver difficulties than these in the way of such a sketch as that which I am now attempting. Some natures, perhaps the happiest, possess the convenient attribute of transparency. Their thoughts, their tastes, their struggles,—each step in their mental and moral development,—are open to all who care to know about them. They are inspired by a frankness—not wholly untinged, perhaps, by vanity — which disposes them to talk about themselves. They break out in autobiographies and personal recollections. As regards their own mental history, such persons have no private life, nor wish to have it. The first-comer is welcome to enter and make himself at home. The biographers of such persons have an easy task. The difficulty begins with natures of less simple texture, and temperaments less unreserved. There are minds which are dominated by an instinctive reserve. They have intellectual and moral recesses, the gloom of which they themselves hardly venture to explore, problems which they give up as insoluble, depths which no plummet may sound, obstinate questionings to which no answer is forthcoming, mysteries of their own consciousness before which they stand in mute bewilderment. The last thing which natures so constituted can endure is the idea of the prying eye and officious tongue, which would destroy the privacy of existence, invade the recesses of thought and feeling, and make their inner life the theme of common talk. To invite the public to walk

in, observe, and criticize, seems to them a sort
of desecration of holy places, which should be
guarded in obscurity. If they have a strong
emotion, their first impulse is to shroud it
from notoriety. Some friendly ear may, in
some especially confidential moment, catch a
hint of that which lies beneath ; but such
flashes of outspokenness are few and far
between. To the world at large the man
remains inscrutable. To the acquaintances of
Society he shows in abundance all that Society
demands — brilliancy, affability, sympathetic
good-nature, amusement. His inner—his real
self—is shrouded in impenetrable reserve. His
fun is often the unconscious artifice of Nature
guarding itself against unwelcome invasion.
With a dexterous hand he guides conversation
away from topics which may aid the invader's
movements. He is an adept in the arts of
polite but effectual resistance to the too eager
familiarity which is inquisitive, and may soon
become impertinent. If he ever unlocks the

secret chambers of his soul, it is under conditions which impose an eternal silence on those who are allowed to enter. How, without betrayal of sacred confidence, can any attempt at the portraiture of such a character be made ?

In Lord Bowen's case the difficulty is enhanced by the circumstance that the two persons best qualified from long and intimate friendship to form a judgment on his life and character passed from the scene within a few weeks of his death. The late Master of Balliol, exercising a discretion which, without questioning, we may be allowed to deplore, directed a holocaust of his papers, and among them perished, it is certain, much that would have exhibited Charles Bowen in one of the most interesting phases of his character—his warm affection and unswerving loyalty to a teacher whom he revered. Lord Coleridge, who early appreciated his brilliant junior's endowments, and who remained on terms of confidential and affectionate intimacy to the end, survived just long enough to learn and mourn his friend's death. He is no longer here to give—as he would, one knows, have given in a delightful form—the result of his lifelong friendship. The loss in either case is irreparable.

No adequate account of Charles Bowen's life and character can, accordingly, be given. None the less, those who loved him and who knew how truly lovable he was, cannot but crave for some lasting embodiment of their remembrance. Little or much as we may have known, or may know, an impression remains, too dear to be allowed to fade. Some definite portrait we must have—however inadequate and unworthy—round which our thoughts may rally, and which may give precision, reality, and life to the floating images which memory—treacherous and wayward servant at the best—brings fitfully before the mind's eye. The physical portrait, faulty and insufficient as the eye of affection feels it to be, is, nevertheless, not without its value. It cannot fill the void—it

cannot lessen the sense of loss; it falls short
in a hundred ways of all that we remember of
the living man. None the less we prize it.
Some such value may, it is hoped, attach to
the attempt to group into a consistent whole,
and embody in a permanent form, some
scattered recollections, which no one who knew
Lord Bowen would willingly let die.

Charles Synge Christopher Bowen was born
January 1, 1835, at Woolaston, a village near
Chepstow, in Gloucestershire, of which his
father, the Rev. Christopher Bowen, had at that
time the curacy. Mr. Bowen came of an Irish
family from County Mayo. In theology he
was a pronounced member of the Evangelical
school. He was a man of exceptional vigour
both in mind and body, of natural gentleness
and calm, and of considerable gifts. He
abounded in amusing stories of the Ireland of
former days. He had a fine voice, was an
excellent reader, and his children enjoyed no
greater treat than to lie on the hearthrug and

listen to his rendering of one of Shakespeare's
plays.   Mr. Bowen was subsequently for some
years curate of the Abbey Church at Bath.
Thence he was transferred to the Rectory of
Southwark, and, subsequently, to St. Thomas's,
Winchester.   Later in life he settled at
Totland, near Freshwater, in the Isle of Wight.
Mr. Bowen, as an Irish proprietor, had suffered
from the famine years, and the family, in its
various homes, lived in frugal fashion.   He
died, in a very hale old age, when on a visit to
the Riviera in 1890.

Charles Bowen's maternal grandmother, Lady
Steele, was a daughter of Count d'Alton, an
Austrian officer of distinction, one of the
Imperial chamberlains at the Court of Joseph
II.   He fell in the trenches of Dunkirk, while
co-operating with an English force against a
French Revolutionary army.   His widow, an
Irish Clancarty by descent, was a fervent
adherent of Marie Antoinette, and much
esteemed in Royalist circles.   She migrated to

England, where her second daughter, Charles Bowen's grandmother, married Sir R. Steele, an Irish baronet, and an officer in the 4th Dragoon Guards, then quartered near Dublin. Lady Steele moved for a while in the society of Dublin and its little court ; but gradually withdrew into a small circle of congenial religious friends, and devoted herself to a life of study and benevolence. She was not slow to recognize her grandson's brilliant promise, and took a lively interest in his school and college career. To her intelligence, seriousness, and strength of will, it is probable that Charles Bowen was indebted for some of his most characteristic gifts.

At ten years of age Charles Bowen was sent to school at Lille, along with his younger brother, Edward. Here the two lads spent a year, learning French and laying the foundation of a polite education. This period of expatriation—necessitated by the mother's broken health—was not altogether a happy

one for the little exiles. The *régime* was
strict, and Charles underwent some harsh
treatment.   There are letters—monthly pro-
ductions, apparently—from Charles to his
father and mother, the phenomenal propriety
and laboured caligraphy of which suggest the
superintendence of a friendly critic's eye.
Charles writes that he has begun Latin, and is
in the second book of the Æneid.   He was
evidently a precocious child.   " I should like,"
he says, "to begin Greek again, for I have
forgotten all but a few words."   Strange utterance for a ten-years-old scholar, which sounds
as if no time had been lost at home in starting
the prize-man of the future on his career of
letters.   He is learning French fables, he tells
his mother, and is progressing favourably in
le dessin.   " I hope that when I shall see you
again, I shall be able to draw pretty well."
The little learners were hard-worked indeed.
" We have ten hours of lessons in the day, and
we have begun geometry, though not in our

own but in another French book, which I do
not like half as well as Euclid. We are obliged
to pronounce the Latin just as we would pronounce our French, which improves it very
much, I think, and which is much better for us,
for it teaches us to read French as well as the
Latin."

There are happily some lighter touches,
more consonant with childhood's wants and
tastes. "On Thursday last," Charles writes,
"we walked to Menin, which is sixteen miles
off; there I bought some skates, and we came
back in a little *voiture* when it was quite dark,
and they did not give us a lantern; therefore
we were nearly upset twice. There is a great
difference between the towns of France and
England, for the towns of France, at least
those of the frontier, are all fortified; and in
England there is no need of all this fortification,
for the sea is enough defence for it."

In a more natural vein is an account of
Madame Marzials' *fête*, which is duly celebrated

by holiday-making, presentation of presents and flowers, a state dinner at half-past three, and a "party" at seven, at which were "all our boys, the professors, and six or seven young ladies. We played blind-man's buff, and a French game called 'Toilette,' which I am just going to explain to you. . . . Thus ended the birthday of Madame Marzials."

"As a child," writes his brother, "he was a great reader, and a very fast one. Our books were few, but very well read. Two volumes of Johnson's complete works were a great treasure, and the 'Rambler' and 'Idler'; of course all Scott, and as much Shakespeare and Spenser as he could understand. But games were, also, never out of his thoughts or his ambitions. He was physically strong and active then and for several years after; in fact, till his law work began. He is the only person I have ever known to jump a cow as it stood."

From Lille, Charles Bowen was sent to Blackheath Proprietary School, where he

remained for three years, learning, amongst
other good things, to be an excellent cricketer.
Here the character and powers of the young
student made themselves distinctly apparent.
In September, 1850, we find the Rev. E. J.
Selwyn, the head-master, writing to Dr.
Goulburn, head-master of Rugby, with reference to Charles's entrance at a public school.
He speaks of his appetite for knowledge in
every branch of learning, and "his capability
for acquiring and digesting and retaining it
as of a very remarkable order." His capa-
bilities had, it would seem, been severely
tested. "Among the subjects he has read
with me," says Mr. Selwyn, "are the ' Hecuba,'
the ' Medea,' and the ' Ajax,' the first book of
Herodotus, a good deal of the ' Cyropædia,'
some of the orations of Demosthenes, several
books of Homer, a good many Idylls of
Theocritus, and the first book of Thucydides ;
and, in Latin, most of Horace, a good many
Orations of Cicero, the third book of the

c

'De Officiis,' nearly the whole of the 'De Oratore,' and, I think, the Georgics. As far as my recollection serves me, this is a tolerably accurate account of his reading, though it does not include all. In composition he is quite as successful as I have ever found boys of his age, and in Latin Elegiacs his advance has been lately rather remarkable : a fatal facility is sometimes his bane in this particular. Indeed, his chief defect is an occasional tendency to inaccuracy, but not at all remarkable in a boy so young and so advanced." He had suffered, Mr. Selwyn thought, "from the absence of the kind of support which the society of active and honourable rivals always furnishes to boys of an aspiring disposition. His temperament is very nervous and excitable : a harsh word will easily disconcert him, and he readily forms attachments to those who are set over him, and will take pride in pleasing them."

"In respect of moral character," Mr. Selwyn

goes on to say, " I would willingly believe that he is even a pious boy; or, if that be a quality beyond the range of our power to certify with perfect security, he is, at least, all that a boy may be short of that. Of the soundness of his principles and the genuineness and sincerity of his motives, I have never had the shadow of a doubt. Of his truthfulness and love of truth in others I have the highest opinion, and I can bear strong testimony to his unflinching adherence to the truth under all circumstances. The excellent manner in which he has been brought up under the immediate and unfailing care of his parents manifests itself in him most conspicuously. I dare not say that he has been tested yet as he will be tested at Rugby, where the temptations and other incentives to err are probably so much greater than at Blackheath. When, however, the time comes that shall try him, I shall indeed be surprised if he be found not to stand the test."

Amply indeed did Charles Bowen justify this

agreeable prophecy. In 1850 he was entered
at Rugby in the School House, then presided
over by Dr. Goulburn, who had, some months
previously, become head-master of the school.
Bowen and several other clever new-comers—
amongst them Robinson Ellis, now Professor
of Latin at Oxford, and T. H. Green, the well-
known tutor at Balliol, were placed in the
Upper Fifth, the highest Form in which the
rules of the school permitted a new boy to
begin his Rugby career. The master of this
Form was Mr. Bradley, the present Dean of
Westminster. Besides his master in Form,
each boy had a private tutor, and the tutor, in
the first instance, selected for Charles Bowen
was the Rev. G. E. L. Cotton, subsequently
Head-master of Marlborough and Bishop of
Calcutta. Mr. Bradley was not long in dis-
covering that it was no ordinary pupil with
whom he had to deal. He describes him as a
boy to whom his heart at once went out—full
of life, energy, and interest in all things, quick

in intellectual movement, voracious in literary appetite—altogether delightfully clever.

" I remember," says Mr. H. T. Rhoades, one of Charles Bowen's school-fellows at Rugby, " his arrival at school. He came in the middle of the term, the evening before the whole holiday, on which nearly every boy made some excursion for the day. I was living in the town, and, as our families were acquainted, I went to the School House to get him to spend the day with us; and, much to my surprise, I found him in the dormitory, reading ' Alcestis ' for his amusement."

At the end of the first half-year, Charles Bowen's and Robinson Ellis's names appeared at the head of the list. This involved their promotion to the " Twenty," a Form which intervened between the Fifth and Sixth. Charles Bowen thus passed from Mr. Bradley's Form instruction. In 1852, however, on Mr. Cotton's appointment to Marlborough, Bowen

became Mr. Bradley's private pupil, and continued to be so for the rest of his Rugby career.
He and seven or eight other pupils were
constantly in their tutor's study.   A close and
intimate friendship was cemented between the
two, and Mr. Bradley obtained a fuller insight
into the young scholar's extraordinary gifts.
"There was," writes Dean Bradley, "a great
power in him of covering quickly a large and
varied field of work.   In this, I have had no
pupil at Rugby who could be compared with
him.   I remember well how, in his last year
and a half, he would bring me his 'Corpus
Poetarum,' and I would suggest to him large
portions of Lucretius, as well as of later poets
—Juvenal, Martial, Lucan, and even Claudian
—for private reading; and I remember the
surprise with which I have received his
request for more, showing me how much he
had contrived to read since he had last consulted me."

Such powers and such diligence produced

the natural result. Honours soon began to
rain apace. In 1853 C. Bowen was successful
in gaining the prize for the Parker Theological
Essay, by a disquisition on "The Several
Parts of Public Worship, and their relation to
each other as illustrated by the Morning and
Evening Services of the Church." Opinions
will differ, probably, as to the wisdom of invit-
ing lads of seventeen to enter upon a grave
theological disquisition, and to display a familiarity with a host of Fathers, Divines, and
other ecclesiastical magnates, which it would
be equally impossible and undesirable that they
should really enjoy. Charles Bowen's essay
was, however, a remarkable performance. The
extraordinary diligence which characterized all
his work was apparent in an imposing array
of authorities ; grave opinions are enumerated
with the solemnity which the occasion demanded, and a rich profusion of theological
lore, skilfully thrown into artistic form, reaped
its appropriate reward in the eulogium of a

learned prelate, the Bishop of Winchester, who wrote to congratulate Mr. Bowen on a son of such fine theological promise.

Other successes were soon to come. In 1854 C. Bowen won the Queen's Medal for Modern History and the prize for a Latin essay. In November, 1853, he went up to Oxford as a candidate for the Balliol Scholarship, and came back to school having achieved this great distinction. "I never before or since," says Dean Bradley, "in my long experience as a schoolmaster, wrote the usual formal testimonial for a pupil of whose success I felt so absolutely certain. He remained at Rugby till the following summer, and was, I need hardly say, quite the heroic figure in the society of his contemporaries. His high spirit, his high principles, his great humour, his prominence in all outdoor school amusements and pursuits, secured him the affection of his friends, and the homage (for it almost amounted to that) of the mass of his school-fellows."

This hero-worship was, no doubt, intensified by an episode which, about this time, presented the young scholar to an admiring world in an attitude which all could appreciate—the physical champion of an injured cause. It was the fashion of that day to call in question the Monitorial System, which Dr. Arnold had established with such marked success at Rugby, and which the other great English schools were hastening to introduce. Prominent among the assailants was the *Daily News*, and a representative of that journal happened to be at Rugby when an incident—of common enough occurrence in school-life—seemed to offer excellent material for a fresh assault. Three little boys—none of them within measurable distance of the Sixth Form—got into a quarrel while out jumping. The quarrel ended in two of them pushing the third into a brook which he could not summon up courage to jump. A grotesque misrepresentation of this childish squabble appeared in the

Daily News, with an appropriate denunciation of the system under which such oppression could occur. Boyish indignation is quickly kindled, and Rugby was very indignant. As ill-luck would have it, Charles Bowen and the guilty newspaper correspondent crossed each other's paths. The school - hero promptly called the calumniator to account. An altercation ensued; and how easy and natural the lapse from words to blows! The man of letters succumbed to the youthful prowess of his assailant, and was forced to retreat, worsted, from the field—worsted, but not resourceless; for the strong arm of the law was invoked, and Charles Bowen's joy of victory was sobered by the arrival of a summons to answer a charge of assault before a bench of Warwickshire magistrates. Things were beginning to look serious; there is extant a letter of Charles Bowen's to his brother, in which he sets out his case with studied moderation, and is evidently anxious as to the impression which

the story might make upon his parents.
Happily the Bench rose to the occasion, appreciated the excessive provocation which had
betrayed the young Rugbeian to a deed of
violence, and imposed a fine so nominal as to
leave no doubt that the defendant's behaviour
was more than half approved. The hero of
the occasion returned to his co-mates more
heroic than ever.

There was, however, plenty of scope at
Rugby for athletic distinctions of a less
equivocal order. Charles Bowen had thrown
himself with ardour into the games of the
place, attained the distinction — dearest of
earthly honours to the schoolboy heart—of a
place in the school Eleven, and become a
redoubtable champion of the football field.
Rugby football was then, as it is now, a somewhat rough form of amusement to those who
took a prominent part in it, well calculated
to stir the combatant to an angry mood.
Nothing, however — not even the heat of

physical encounter — could ruffle Bowen's urbanity, the sweetness of his temper. One of the combatants in those Homeric struggles still recalls the "angelic smile" with which Bowen, after carrying discomfiture into the enemy's ranks, and being himself the object of many rude assaults, would emerge from the fiercest football scrimmage.

About this time Charles Bowen was within measurable distance of becoming a soldier, a profession in which throughout life he took a lively interest, and for which he always felt a strong predilection. The war with Russia— the tragic excitements of Crimean battle-fields —were firing the blood of the youth of England, and Dean Bradley relates how, when a certain number of commissions were placed by the War Office at the disposal of the head-master, Bowen was sorely exercised in mind by the temptation of a military career. Some overtures to his father on the subject encountered, we may believe, a discouraging reception, for

the idea was ultimately abandoned.   Bowen
was now too hard at work to indulge in day-
dreams, military or other.   His teachers, however, appear sometimes to have tried his
temper.   In a book of notes, taken under Dr.
Goulburn's instruction, occurs a little outbreak
of impatience.   " I protest," writes the young
student, "against taking these notes, and
solemnly declare that I take them only under
physical compulsion."   Despite such occasional
lapses, Charles Bowen proved himself a model
scholar.   In June, 1854, he left Rugby, his
honours thick upon him.   His crowning
achievement was to win the First Exhibition,
the examiners adding " Facile Princeps" to
his name.   His fame still lives in Rugby
tradition.   "What impressed his contemporaries," says Mr. H. T. Rhoades, "was the
union of brilliance and sound qualities with
great athletic powers.   He gained the cup
held by the winner of the greatest number of
"events" in the athletic games, and he was,

without exception, the finest football-player I remember."

Professor Robinson Ellis, Charles Bowen's friend and most formidable competitor at Rugby, furnishes some interesting reminiscences of their careers—of struggles in which victory fell sometimes to one, sometimes to the other; of the resolution of each—successfully accomplished—to break the spell which for seven years had denied to Rugby the honour of a Balliol Scholarship; and of tragic vicissitudes which shook the calm of schoolboy life: such, for instance, as Bowen's failure to win a Latin poem prize, which public opinion had accorded to him, owing to a critical objection taken by the composition master to the expression "auratum Oriona," which Bowen had coined out of the Virgilian line—

"Armatum que auro circumspicit Oriona,"

an abbreviation which his critic denounced as "unclassical and impossible," and which was instrumental in transferring the prize to a candidate of whom no one had ever thought.

"A wave of High Church sentiment was," Professor Ellis says, "at this time passing over Rugby School." Goulburn, who succeeded Dr. Tait, in 1850, had introduced many of the ritualistic innovations, which were then the symbols of Tractarianism. A Roman Catholic Church had recently been raised in a conspicuous spot adjoining the playing-fields; three Rugby boys were believed to have " gone over," and sixth-form enthusiasts began to dream of possible reunion with Rome. Bowen showed but slight sympathy with the prevailing mood; nor was he impressed by the miracles recorded by William of Malmesbury, and Bede, whose chronicles had been admitted for study in the Sixth Form in lieu of the ordinary Greek or Latin history. "In 1852," says Professor Ellis, "table-turning became all the rage, and a passion for magnetic experiments invaded Rugby. We turned tables in our studies, and

even in our bedrooms, and tried our magnetiz-
ing powers on each other. In this Bowen was
remarkably successful. His eyes were strong
and penetrating, and he succeeded in putting
many of the boys on whom he experimented
into a state of coma." Happily for the nerves
of all parties, the head-master intervened, and
put an end to this dangerous form of excitement.

Charles Bowen went up to Oxford with all
the prestige of a Balliol Scholarship, a first-rate
school reputation for ability, and—still dearer
dignity in schoolboys' eyes—a well-established
fame in the athletic world. The boyish
traditions, which grow so generously around a
successful and popular comrade, heralded his
advent. Oxford received him with open arms.
At Balliol he was especially welcome. The
student set rejoiced in an accession which
was certain to confer lustre on the College
and the University. Cricketers hailed a
valuable reinforcement to the ranks. The
devotees of football, which the Rugby game

was helping to bring into fashion, had heard of his prowess, and knew that a mighty man had come amongst them. All alike found in the new-comer a delightful acquisition for every gathering, where the charm of companionship could be quickened by high spirits, geniality, wit that played but never wounded, and fun that knew no touch of coarseness.

There was a prejudice in those days against a somewhat pretentious superiority, which the Rugby system was supposed to engender, and which did not tend to conciliate outsiders. The Rugby monitor was supposed to pride himself on his "moral thoughtfulness;" a scoffing world denounced him as a prig. There were those who thought that they discovered in Charles Bowen, on his first arrival at Oxford, a touch of this Rugbeian temper, lurking under an almost deferential urbanity of manner. If it were so, it speedily disappeared under the wholesome influences of the larger world to which he now belonged. No one was ever

D

less anxious to pose as superior. His aim
seemed rather to keep his superiority, well out
of sight.

Life at the University, to those who enter
upon it with Charles Bowen's advantages, is
among the halcyon periods of human existence.
Its freedom alike from the petty discipline
of school, and the anxieties of after-life, its
absorbing interests, its varied enjoyments,
its wide and unexplored fields of intellectual
adventure, as the serious aims and pursuits of
life break gradually into view; the opportunities for friendship which present themselves
on every hand, and the capacity for hero-
worship which such opportunities enkindle;
last, and not least, the inspiring genius of the
place, its solemn beauty and charm, make up
a whole which, to a sensitive and congenial
temperament, scarcely falls short of fascination.
Charles Bowen entered with avidity upon the
new and delightful chapter of his life. It was
an exciting atmosphere for so ardent a nature

to breathe. The old Conservative tastes and
traditions of Oxford and the new spirit of
Liberalism were meeting, like two opposing
currents, and seething in conflict. Reform
was in the air, but there were many to whom
Reform implied the shock of all that was
dearest and most sacred. The great theological movement, which had stirred the preceding generation, had sunk into comparative
quiescence. John Henry Newman no longer
entranced an audience at Littlemore. The
last of the distinguished Oxford converts had
passed the uncertain frontier which separated
the domains of the Roman and Anglican
Churches. Religious controversy was no
longer the topic of the hour, and was tabooed
at social gatherings. The affectation of
Roman modes of thought and Roman ceremonial had ceased to be in vogue, and was
even liable to a little contemptuous persecution. The Reform movement of the earlier
years of the century, which the High Church

reaction for a while superseded, had resumed
its course. To the theological movement had
succeeded another, with as serious a spirit and
an even wider scope. There were leading
spirits at Oxford, who saw that the English
Universities had fallen from their original
ideal, and were missing their true function as
national centres of education. They were
courageous innovators. They had resolved
not only that Oxford should open her gates to
the nation at large ; but that her teaching and
system should be brought into touch with the
wants, convictions, and difficulties of modern
England. She should no longer continue to
be the stronghold of obsolete methods, the
rallying-point of respectable abuses, the home,
as Mr. Bright said, of dead languages and
undying prejudices, but should become a
great instrument for moulding the character
and guiding the lives of the on-coming generation, and, through it, of the nation at large.
Her sons were to be sent out—not mere

Churchmen or scholars—but fully equipped for the struggle to which their age would commit them — in intelligent sympathy with their fellow-strugglers, fitted to appreciate and to co-operate with all that was best, truest, and highest in modern life. Among the centres, where the spirit of reform made itself especially felt, was Balliol College. Dr. Jenkyns, the Master, a vigorous and far-sighted administrator—despite some foibles and eccentricities with which his contemporaries were accustomed to make merry—had been laying, deep and strong, the foundations of the future greatness of the College. He was insistent in improving wherever improvement seemed possible, in perfecting the discipline and education of the place, and in collecting, for the purpose, a group of tutors whose zeal and abilities were destined, at no distant date, to carry Balliol to the foremost rank as a seat of learning. Prominent among them was Benjamin Jowett, whose influence on those who came within his

reach had been felt, year by year, in an ever-
widening circle, though still narrow as compared with that of later times. At present he
was chiefly known to the outside world as a
courageous and original thinker, and as the
advocate of views on various theological topics,
which were regarded in orthodox circles as
dangerous innovations. His Commentary on
Three Pauline Epistles seemed to the general
English reader — whom, in those days, the
research and learned speculations of Germany
had scarcely reached—to mark the initiative of
a revolutionary epoch in Biblical interpretation.
Such a man makes his influence felt on friend
and foe. The upholders of plenary and literal
inspiration—and they were neither few nor
uninfluential—were scandalized and alarmed.
The echoes of the controversy fluttered the
dovecots of many a snug common-room and
quiet country parsonage. A few years later,
Jowett emphasized his position as a reformer
by his participation in a collection of " Essays

and Reviews," which speedily became notorious as a quasi-authoritative announcement of a progressive propaganda in matters theological. The frightened champions of orthodoxy are not apt to be too scrupulous in their attacks on a supposed heresiarch. Some of the attacks on Jowett were, to say the best of them, ungenerous, and aroused the sympathetic indignation of his friends. The well-meaning combatants, who flocked up to Oxford from country parishes to vote against the endowment of Jowett's Chair, forgot that to curtail an author's salary is not an effectual method of refuting him. The attempted persecution of Jowett, at any rate, appealed to all that was generous in the undergraduate mind. Bowen early became, and remained throughout, his warm ally. It was inevitable that the two men should become close friends. Jowett found in Bowen the ideal student of his hopes and vows. Bowen became, year by year, more impressed with the Master's excellence, wisdom,

and far-reaching kindness.   His friendship for
Jowett, and the sincere loyalty and devotion
with which he regarded him, were, I believe,
among the one or two most powerful external
influences which moulded Charles Bowen's
tastes and sympathies and shaped the course
of his life.

Another of the tutors was Lake, the present
Dean of Durham, an accomplished scholar
of a different caste of thought from that of
Jowett, and exercising a less active personal
influence on undergraduates.   Among the
junior tutors were Riddell, a bright, charming,
saintly character, well equipped with the
refined scholarship for which Shrewsbury
School was justly famed ; and Edwin Palmer,
the late Archdeacon of Oxford, younger
brother of the late Lord Selbourne—one of a
trio of brothers of whose attainments Oxford
is justly proud.   Henry Smith was lecturer
in mathematics, and was loyally devoting his
extraordinary powers to the task of education.

Bowen at a later date became his pupil, and, at the time of his death, bore testimony in language of fitting beauty to the almost unique combination of moral and intellectual excellencies which presented itself in this splendidly endowed nature.*

It was no small privilege, certainly, which the members of Balliol at this period enjoyed. It had become the custom to invite such of the unsuccessful candidates as had attracted notice in the Scholarship Examinations, to enter the college as commoners; and Balliol thus gathered to itself the flower of the public schools, and contained a class of men distinctly above the average of undergraduate ability.

Amongst the Balliol men of Bowen's own standing were Newman, a serious and profound student, the promise of whose early career was,

* The article in the *Spectator*, reprinted as "Recollections by Lord Bowen" among the "Biographical Sketches of Henry J. S. Smith" (Oxford : Clarendon Press), is an excellent specimen of Bowen's style in journalism.

unhappily, clouded by a breakdown of health ; Merry, ὀρθῶς ἐπώνυμος, whose lot at a much later stage it was, as Public Orator, to commemorate Charles Bowen's death among the losses of the year ; Blomfield, a son of the Bishop of London, himself in later years a bishop, endowed with an hereditary aptitude for classical niceties, and a dry and caustic wit ; Warre, the present Head-master of Eton, in those days much renowned as a sturdy oarsman and cricketer ; E. Herbert, a young man of rare charm and promise, who became political *attaché* at Athens, and met a tragic fate at the hands of brigands at Marathon.

Among Charles Bowen's more intimate college friends were Austen Leigh, now Rector of Wargrave ; Alexander Craig Sellar, of whose services in and out of Parliament the Liberal Unionist party has so grateful a recollection ; and Bullock-Hall, now the hospitable lord of Six Mile Bottom, who had formed on the Rugby cricket-ground a friendship with

Bowen, which became confirmed at college,
and lasted, in undiminished vigour, to the end.
W. G. Cole, now Rector of Newbold Verdun,
in Leicestershire, was at this time a scholar of
Trinity; the separation of colleges, however,
had done nothing to impair the warm affection
which had grown up between the two at
Rugby, and which continued unabated throughout life. Of senior men outside the college,
who formed a part of Charles Bowen's surroundings there were, besides Henry Smith,
Sir Alexander Grant, renowned as an expositor
of Aristotelian philosophy; T. C. Sandars, an
expert in Roman law, who was on several occasions Bowen's tutor, one of the men of whose
rare gifts of wit, learning, and wisdom the
world never knows, but who for many years
contributed to enrich the periodical literature
of his country; George Brodrick, the genial
and accomplished Warden of Merton, who
had known Bowen from childhood, and to
whose recollections of his friend I have been

largely indebted in the preparation of the present sketch. Horace Davey had already established a reputation, which his professional career has not belied, and was displaying in the schools the intellectual prowess which has carried him to the House of Lords. John Conington, though much of a recluse, was widely known and admired as among the most accomplished Latinists of his day; and Goldwin Smith, master of a style of unsurpassed brilliancy and force, was warring fiercely upon all—friend or foe—who had the misfortune to provoke his somewhat indiscriminate combativeness. Arthur Butler, no unworthy member of a family of scholars, was widely esteemed for culture and geniality; George Goschen, leader of distinguished Rugbeians, was hurried away from academic triumphs to no less pronounced eminence in the world of politics and finance; and Charles Pearson, an Oriel Fellow of distinction, whose failing health, a few years later, drove him to

Australia, where he rose high in the sphere of education and politics, and gathered, it must be feared, from a somewhat gruesome experience, the materials for the gloomy vaticinations of the future of humanity with which he startled Society a year or two ago. At Wadham Richard Congreve had for years been making his presence felt as a man of courageous thought, strong grasp, and intellectual acumen. He was an acknowledged authority on historical subjects, and had gathered around him a small but distinguished circle of admirers, who became in later years the interpreters to their country of the doctrines of Comte, and the protagonists of Positivism.

An atmosphere charged with intellectual and spiritual forces so powerful and so conflicting, was not likely to remain long undisturbed. The new ideas craved expression. The series of "Oxford Essays," edited by T. C. Sandars, made its first appearance in 1854, and struck a new note of literary activity. Henry

Smith, in his essay on the plurality of worlds, boldly challenged the great authority of Whewell, and gave the world a foretaste of his extraordinary gifts. A few years later the plan of the "Oxford Essays" was abandoned; but in "Essays and Reviews" a more systematic attempt was made to liberalize English theology, to enlarge the limits of the freedom which clergymen of the English Church might lawfully enjoy, and, especially, to place Biblical criticism and the whole theory of Biblical interpretation on a sounder and more intelligent basis. A writer in the *Edinburgh Review*—himself a redoubtable champion of any cause in which religious freedom was concerned—has given a graphic account of the fierce controversy which ensued, and the sort of panic which spread through the ranks of the more conservative order of Churchmen. It gradually became apparent that much which the authors of "Essays and Reviews" alleged — however startling to the uninformed—had long been familiar to erudite theologians, and had even been avowed by them, though in language less aggressively crude. Some needlessly offensive phrases demanded apology; but when these had been condoned, the result was found not to transcend the liberty of judgment accorded by the Church of England to her ministers.

While these high combats shook the upper air, the tide of practical reform was flowing in lower regions with a force and rapidity which struck timorous obstructives with consternation. One by one, in rapid succession, the traditional safeguards began to totter, to crumble, to disappear. A Royal Commission threw wide the gates of the University to all who wished to enter, irrespective of creed. The obligation of celibacy, which had given to the tutorial body something of a conventual character, was treated as an obsolete survival of monasticism. The monopolizing supremacy of classics and philosophy as topics of education was successfully disputed. Logic, and the refinements of

the School-men began to wear a pedantic and
mediæval air. Physical science, in all the
audacity and self-confidence of youth, boldly
asserted her claims, and the Aristophanic
sarcasm, Δῖνος βασιλεύει τὸν Δί ἐξεληλακώς,
seemed in course of realization. There was,
naturally, much alarm, and something of the
indiscriminating antagonism which alarm en-
genders. Fierce assaults were delivered at
any point which seemed assailable. Stanley
and Jowett stood out as obvious objects of
attack. "Jowett-baiting," writes Sir Mount-
Stuart Grant-Duff, "was, indeed, the favourite
amusement of the united forces of Anglo-
Catholic, High and Dry Anglican, and Evangelical Parsondom. I remember that, on one
occasion, I think in 1864, we were all summoned to go down to vote in Convocation
about some changes in the curriculum. Shortly
afterwards we were again summoned, as a
grand Jowett-bait was impending in the same
august assembly. Some one in the train, on

the way to Oxford, said, 'I really think that we may win to-day about Jowett's salary. The country clergy came up in such numbers to vote about that educational question, that they will hardly go to the trouble and expense of coming again.' 'Won't they?' said Bowen; 'they will think that education is a bad thing, but that justice is a worse, and they will come in hundreds,' which was precisely what they did."

This story, though belonging to a somewhat later stage of Charles Bowen's career, well illustrates the influences which were acting on him from the outset of his University life. He found around him, on all hands, men bent on improvement, eager to remove inequalities and disabilities, anxious to throw open to the nation at large the advantages which had hitherto been the monopoly of a privileged class. In another sphere he saw new aspects of theological opinion presented with all the force of research, ability, and

E

insight, and confronted by an opposition
which—if it may be said without disrespect—
was not always intelligent, generous, or well
informed.   Opinion has marched so fast the
last forty years, that it is not easy to realize
the   position from   the   standpoint   of the
oncoming generation of that day, and the
alternatives which presented themselves for
acceptance.   I remember, for instance, hearing
a distinguished member of his party, preaching
to   the   University in St.   Mary's Church,
advance with vehemence the proposition that
the Christian religion, indeed all religious
belief, would be fatally undermined if the
authority or authenticity of a single word,
"a jot or tittle," of the accepted canon were
allowed to be called in question.   Another
leader, justly eminent as orator and scholar,
devoted his fine powers to explaining to the
undergraduate conscience the grounds on
which the Athanasian Creed must be regarded
as an essential part of the Christian's panoply,

and an unfailing source of peace and joy to
the reflective mind. On another occasion a
much-esteemed prelate enforced the wavering
orthodoxy of his audience by the stern truth
that errors of opinion were, if sin was to be
weighed against sin, sins of a deeper dye and
involving graver consequences to the sinner
than mere peccadillos against morality.

Compare views such as these with Professor
Jowett's erudite and deeply considered essays
on Biblical authority, and on the true purport
of "Inspiration," or with the generous appreciation of excellence and nobility which
breathes through every line that Stanley
wrote, and can it be a matter of surprise that
undergraduates of Charles Bowen's temperament should have espoused with enthusiasm
the cause, as it seemed to them, of justice,
truth, and common sense? Charles Bowen
became and remained for life a reformer;
remained, too, the affectionate disciple and
friend of the man who bore the main brunt

of the encounters, and enjoyed the chief honours of the persecution—Benjamin Jowett.

Bowen's list of academical successes was a long one. In 1855 he succeeded, at his first trial, in winning the "Hertford," the blue ribbon of Latin scholarship at Oxford. Two years later he won the "Ireland," the other great classical distinction of the University.

His letter to his friend Cole, in reply to a letter of congratulation on this achievement, will be appreciated by Balliol men, who re-member the College jokes to which it refers.

" DEAR COLE,
        "Many thanks for your very acceptable letter of congratulation, which made good fortune itself more agreeable. It is these little tokens of epistolary intercourse which set the seal of heaven upon the sea of life. I was, of course, much pleased to hear of the result of the examination, which I did as I was a-playing rackets with M. Pattison, in the identical court where I was fortunate enough to hear of the Hertford. It was after a brilliant and extraordinary manœuvre of that learned individual, resembling in all important particulars a series of

charges of the heaviest cavalry, that Palmer appeared at the door with gladness in his gaze. The following conversation of the most exciting and intense nature then ensued, strictly resembling that which used actually to occur at the most important crises of Greek life.

Palmer. ἀνδρὲς φίλοι τὸ πρῶτον ἀγγείλαι θέλω—

Bowen. τέθνηκε —— ; τοῦτο βούλομαι μαθεῖν.

Palmer. οὐκ· ἀλλὰ σάκκους αἰὲν ἀρχαίους * νέμει·

Bowen. μῶν λευκὸς ἐξόλωλεν αἴλουρος χρόνῳ ;

Palmer. ἀλλαντοπώλοι ζῶντα προσβλέπουσι νίν·

Bowen. τί δ' οὖν, σάφες μοι μῆκος ἐκτείνον λόγου.

Palmer. θέλεις ἀκούειν πάνθ' ἅμ' ἐξειρήμενα·

Bowen. τί μὴ θέλουσι θ' ἅτερον προβάλλεται.

Palmer. ἕως ἂν ἐκμάθῃς πότ' ἡσύχως ἐχεῖν.

" Here followed two or three pages of beautiful and polished Greek dialogue, at the end of which Palmer observed—

' Εἰβερνίαν σύνισθι σοι κεκτημένῳ.'

" Chorus of animated M. Pattisons, in slightly inferior Greek to that which formed the medium of communication between the celebrated individuals above.

Ἰοῦ, ἰοῦ, ἰοῦ μάλα δή·
τί σε προσείπ, τί δέ σοι λέξω ;
ὦ εὐδαίμων σοι συγχαίρω·
ἰοῦ, ἰοῦ ἀγορεύων, κ.τ.λ.

---

* Ancient bags, *i.e.* trousers.

"I should at once, 'belovyed partnier of myyeuthfule jeoys and seorrows,' have written to you, but had no time, and made sure you would see it in the papers. However, I never looked for a note from you in return.   I hope you will be at the O. R. match.

"Ever yours affectionately,

"C. BOWEN.

"P.S.—Are you coming to the Lakes ? If you don't, I shall simply stay at Oxford all the Long, with my scout and the porter's boy."

In the same year Bowen was the successful competitor for the Chancellor's Prize for Latin verse. The poem, for the composition of which Bowen had with characteristic diligence equipped himself by specially reading through six books of the " Æneid," was pronounced by competent judges to rank among the most brilliant of its class.   It achieved, at any rate, the honour of being attentively listened to and much appreciated by the undergraduate portion of the audience in the Sheldonian Theatre.   Its subject was " Sebastopolis." The episodes of the Crimean War were still fresh in the minds of all. Its grave anxieties, its mishaps, its sorrows, still ached in the national recollection. Its successes had flushed the country with a martial joy unknown since the days of Waterloo. Bowen instinctively made the most of an interesting theme. No one who was present will have forgotten the frequent bursts of applause which interrupted the recital. Among the passages thus honoured was a spirited description of the battle of Inkerman.

> " O patria, O fluctu procul Anglia tuta marino,
> Ter crebro numerosa phalanx pede, certa triumphi,
> Irruerat : ter succurrit tua dulcis imago,
> Firmavitque tuos, victum et vi reppulit hostem."

Great, too, was the enthusiasm aroused by the allusion to Miss Nightingale and her beneficent labours in the hospitals of Scutari.

> " Quale melos, vergente die, languentibus olim
> Pectoribus venit atque oculos componit inertes,
> Talis, ubi siccos ardens sitis hauserat artus,
> Adfuit, en, voluit que viris succurrere virgo.
> Ut placidum tulit alma pedem, fugere tenebræ,

Fugit ibi dolor omnis, et irritus avolat angor.
Illa refert somnos et temperat arida labra,
Aut iter extremum submotâ nocte serenat,
Atque mori docet exceptatque novissima verba."

Among the circles where Bowen was most
welcome was a small literary club, which had
been founded in 1852, with the object of
bringing together congenial spirits and promoting more serious and interesting talk than
was easy in the ordinary intercourse of Oxford
life. The original members were three Rugbeians, G. J. Goschen, C. Pearson, and A. G.
Butler; three Etonians, C. S. Parker, W. H.
Fremantle, and G. Brodrick; and one
Harrovian, H. N. Oxenham. We met after
Hall at each other's rooms, enjoyed the
temperate festivities of an Oxford Common
Room, listened to each other's essays with
patience, and discussed them with animation.
Though the club's life was longer than the
Fates usually accord in such cases, it never
found a name to its liking. It rejected with
scorn the depreciatory *sobriquet* of " Mutual

Improvement Society," which its enemies suggested; it hesitated before the Bacchic significance of "Sublime Port," proposed, I think, by Mr. G. Goschen, as inadequate and misleading. Name or no name, it fostered a pleasant freemasonry among its members, and was the pretext for many agreeable gatherings. Bowen in the best possible spirits, interested in everything and longing to discuss it, ingenious, subtle, ironical, vivacious, and quick as lightning in retort, was an invaluable ingredient for such symposia, and was seen there in his happiest vein. His fun would sometimes recall us from a sphere too tremendously metaphysical for mortal intellect. But no one soared into those empyrean heights on bolder wing, or bent a keener gaze on each new range of thought as it opened before us.

In a set of Alcaics, sent to Cole in 1857, Bowen laments with mock pathos a symposium of the Essay Society at his rooms, which interfered with a projected visit to his friend.

The phrase, "Mutui Sapientes," refers, of course, to the mutual improvement which the enemies of the Society declared to be its proper function.

> " O Cole, Coli progenies patris !
> O melle multo suavior, et tamen
> Ventis magis velox acerbis,
> Sollicitos cruciare amicos !
>
> " Diu dolentem spes recreaverat,
> Favoris aurâ jam viduum tui,
> Dum fata cras spero benigna,
> Care, tuas aditurus ædes.
>
> " Eheu ! caducæ spes hominum nimis,
> Et spreta ventis vota furentibus !
> Quam sæpe crudelis voluntas
> Dissociat pia corda Divûm.
>
> " Cras est bibendum cum Sapientibus
> Et danda Bacchi munera Mutuis,
> Cras quicquid Intellectuale est
> Conveniet mea tecta noctu.
>
> " Ænigma vitæ cras meditantibus
> Solvetur : et, cum Tempore, Veritas
> Vanescet Objectiva tandem
> Et Spatii ratio fugacis.
>
> " Ignosce amico, tu tamen, Ah, tuo,
> Fesso perenni jam sapientiâ—
> Quæ pœna tam crudelis ulla est,
> Quanta tuo caruisse visu ? "

Bowen used occasionally to speak at the
Union Debating Society, and in 1858 was
its President. I do not remember, however,
that he ever took it quite seriously enough to
become a distinguished debater. The Warden
of Merton recalls an occasion on which, not
altogether to the taste of his hearers, he
inveighed indignantly against the courtesies
interchanged between Queen Victoria and
Napoleon III. during the Crimean War.

"Among those who were contemporaries of
the late Lord Justice at Oxford, and also took
part in the Debates," writes Mr. H. A. Morrah,
"were John Oakley, of Brasenose, afterwards
Dean of Manchester; King Smith of the same
college, a man held in some esteem as a speaker;
Mitchinson, of Pembroke, now Assistant-
Bishop of Peterborough; Elliot, now Dean of
Windsor, who supplied the earnest and solemn
element. But it was A. V. Dicey, of Balliol,
who shared with Bowen the honour of debate
in the opinion of the critical. Dicey, however,

was hard to hear and difficult to follow, and his methods were different in the extreme from the lucid and mellifluous flow of Bowen's argument."

Bowen, it appears, formed one of several Rugby Presidents whose unbroken succession to this dignified post excited the jealousy of the other great schools. "His portrait hangs in the fine new hall—built some thirty years after he left Oxford—among those of many predecessors and successors honoured in Church and State."

In the year 1857 an unexpected honour awaited him. "You will be glad to hear," he writes to his mother, "that I have been in, on the sly, for our Fellowship examination without telling you, . . . and am elected Fellow of Balliol. Fancy my being a Fellow! Ellis, an old Rugby friend of mine, was my antagonist. I found that I had a legal right to stand, having been elected Scholar before the new Act passed." The same distinction had been conferred on Jowett, while still an undergraduate, in 1838.

In the Class List of Easter Term, 1858, Charles Bowen's name appeared in the First Class, some of his compeers being A. Dicey, now Vinerian Professor of English Law, and a justly valued champion of the Unionist party; John Percival, now Bishop of Hereford; T. E. Holland, Chichele Professor of International Law; and E. Wodehouse, the much-esteemed member for Bath. The examination had not been without its anxieties. At the outset, Bowen had the misfortune to disable his right hand by a fall from his horse, and it was feared that his inability to write would interfere seriously with his paper work in the schools. The difficulty was got over by permission being accorded to Mr. A. Austen Leigh to write Bowen's answers at his dictation, a friendly office which was not, apparently, without its attendant difficulties. "He and I and one examiner," writes Mr. A. Austen Leigh, "sat in a School by ourselves—the School generally used for *vivâ voce* examinations—and for hour after

hour 1 wrote till my hand ached. It was up-
hill work for him, who wrote as quickly as he
thought, and was not accustomed to dictate his
thoughts ; and what made it worse for him, was
the terrible hash which I made of his many
quotations from Greek and Latin authors.
Again and again he had to stop and repeat
them until I understood them, and sometimes
he would dash a finger or a pencil across one
which I could not make come right. In spite
of much provocation, he never lost his temper.
Writing out his answers was certainly a revela-
tion to me, and it showed me, at any rate, what
should be aimed at when my own time should
come."

"Bowen was already a scholar of Balliol,"
writes Austen Leigh, "when I went up in
1855, and it was not till the next year that my
friendship with him dates. My steering the
'Torpid' boat, in which he rowed, and playing
in the eleven with him, brought us together,
and during 1857, 1858, and 1859 we were close

friends. He was a many-sided man, and his striking abilities and his interest in purely intellectual matters did not prevent him caring for and loving one who was more to the front in games than in the Schools.

" Perhaps Alexander Sellar was the connecting-link. He and Bowen were as brothers, or closer than brothers; and Sellar and I were friends. To hear Bowen and Sellar together in those days was a treat never to be forgotten. Sellar, humorous, hard-headed, good-tempered, but sometimes a little crusty, and with thoughts full of brightness, but, perhaps, now and then moving somewhat clumsily; and Bowen, quick, bright, playful, darting round him and striking in, as it were, sharp pins of chaff and fun, till he made him roar, half in anger and half in enjoyment; delighted if he could trip him up or make him flounder in rejoinder, and yet never carrying a joke too far, or provoking loss of temper. That was a distinguishing trait of Bowen's character — his unfailing

kindness and consideration.   He never lost his
own temper, and was never the cause of others
losing theirs."

Bowen's series of academic successes was
concluded in 1859 by the Arnold Historical
Prize.   The competition for this honour is
open to a later stage of University life than is
permitted in the generality of cases, and the
essays are, as a rule, no longer the "declama-
tions" of schoolboys, but the riper reflections
of scholars who have completed the University
curriculum, and have been able to approach
their subject with some degree of leisure and
research.   Charles Bowen's prize essay on
" Delphi, considered locally, morally, and politi-
cally," was no exception to the rule.   It
attracted much attention by beauty of language,
wide and varied learning, poetic feeling, and
keen historical instinct.   It showed how great
a space the famous shrine occupied in con-
temporary society—how it was "to the Hellenic
world what Rome was to the Middle Ages—

the heart of its religion, the source of its culture, the nucleus of its politics. There the influence was enshrined which educated Greek thought, moulded Greek manners, and animated Greek art. The introduction of the faith of the Pythian Apollo was an epoch, a revolution. With that faith Greece grew, and, it may be, the same causes which led to its decline paved the way also for the fall of Greece."

The origin of the shrine is next delineated, the civilizing stream of Dorian migration forcing its way southwards across the plain of Thessaly, carrying with it the worship of the bright god Apollo, and coming into fierce conflict with a primitive religion, whose ascendency it threatened. It was at Delphi that the battle was hottest and most protracted ; the legendary lore of Greece is coloured with the traces of the fight. As the mists of legend melt into the daylight of history, we find Delphi no little city, struggling for existence, but "the Mecca, the Jerusalem of a great

F

kingdom, the Holy City where the tribes go
up to worship." We have next a picturesque
description of the *locale* of the sanctuary,
standing on the highest of a series of terraces
in an amphitheatre between the ridges of the
Parnassus range as they slope seawards. Here
a Dorian priestly aristocracy established itself,
armed with despotic powers of life and death,
levying a splendid revenue from the tenants of
the Temple, and, like the wealthy monasteries
of a later age, provoking an occasional scandal
by their luxury and the tribe of idle mendicants
whom their promiscuous bounty attracted. We
are carried through each stage of the world-
famed oracle, till it reaches its culminating
point as the most powerful moral influence of
the age. Then comes the period of decay.
The world has outgrown the stage at which
prophecy was necessary for the conveyance
of religious dogma and consolation. Its place
was being filled by philosophy. Solon and
Lycurgus had sat at the feet of Apollo, but

the modern statesman looked to his own good
sense for guidance. Suspicions of the purity
of the oracle began to be generally entertained.
The splendid donation of Crœsus was fatal to
the Pythia's reputation. The oracle became less
and less of a moral force, more and more a
political expedient. When the great trial with
Persia arrived, the oracle spoke only to dis-
courage patriotic resistance; and it was the
glory of the Athenians that they "regarded
not the tempting prophecies which emanated
from Delphi, but, swearing to be free, repulsed
the barbarian." Other causes of degradation
were at work. A class of professional soothsayers brought the art of divination into
popular disrepute, and Aristophanes held up
the wandering mendicant to the laughter of
the Athenians. The temples began to be
deserted. There was a general conviction
that Delphi sold its favours to the highest
bidder.

When the next great crisis arrived, it was

found that the Macedonian upstart had secured
the good-will of the oracle. A whisper of
indignation breathed the conviction that the
Python had been "be-Philipped." Philip,
having used the oracle for his own purposes,
showed it the same scanty reverence that
Napoleon showed the Pope, and the darkness
gathered thicker upon the expiring shrine. The
Pythia's utterances grew rare. After the Roman
conquest she became, on all national topics,
mute. Successive invaders pillaged her
treasury. When Nero ransacked it, it had
undergone the same fate eleven times before.
Fitfully, from time to time, its voice is heard
amid the din of flatterers and soothsayers. It
spoke after honour bade it cease. "The last
blow fell when the sacred tripod was taken
to adorn the hippodrome of the new metropolis
of the East. From that time forth the oracle
was dumb."

Studious as Charles Bowen could be, he had
no touch of the book-worm. No man was ever

more alive to the pleasures which are to be
enjoyed outside of schools and libraries. His
prowess in athletics, his robust frame, his
correct eye, his firm hand, made games a
delight. The light-heartedness of youth, health,
and success broke out in healthy good-fellow-
ship. At his college there still live traditions
of whist-parties, whose long-drawn-out sweetness stretched far into the night, and rendered
the conventional attendance at chapel next
morning an achievement of difficulty; and of
an unsuccessful attempt on the part of some
joyful spirits to secure the desired result by
sitting up all night. Virtuous attempt, defeated,
alas! in Charles Bowen's case, by the infirmity
of Nature, which betrayed him into a nap at
the very moment when it was necessary to
put in an appearance.

The earlier portion of Bowen's Oxford life
was largely devoted to enjoyment. But as
time went on, and the final struggle of University
life loomed in the near horizon, he began to

labour more and more assiduously to equip himself for the great ordeal. In no one, assuredly, was the definition of genius as "the faculty of taking pains," more strikingly exemplified. At school, at college, and, afterwards, in professional life, the pains which Bowen took about everything to which he set his hand were infinite. Some of his notebooks, still extant, are miracles of diligence and exactness. The veriest drudge that ever plodded a laborious path to mediocrity could not have recorded his knowledge in more considered form, or systematized it with more elaborate precision. Page after page of minute and exquisite handwriting attest the thoroughness of his mastery of every subject which he came across, and the splendid equipment which carried him to victory in so many intellectual encounters. No toil was spared in arranging, co-ordinating, and setting forth everything that had to be learnt and remembered, in its concisest and most lucid form. A well-worn set of cards, covered with an analysis of "leading cases," while he was a law-student in London, remains as evidence of the indefatigable diligence with which his mind, working at a rate which filled his companions with wonder, could yet stop to make sure of each new step, and to lay the foundation of that varied and extensive knowledge of Law which the Master of the Rolls, in the panegyric pronounced after Lord Bowen's death, described as so remarkable. His note-books at college appear to have been kept on a similar system, and with the same indefatigable exactness.

A letter written by Charles Bowen, in January of this year (1857), to his friend A. Austen Leigh, gives an amusing account of his life at Oxford during the Vacation, when he was staying up to read with Mark Pattison, and of the impressions made upon him by Jowett at an early stage of their acquaintance.

" I have been staying up here diligently reading the Ethics. Of course I went down for Christmas Day,

and returned the day after, finding nobody left in
college but J. King, the white cat, and the coal-heaver,
all, I am happy to say, in tolerable health and spirits.
I am coaching with M. Pattison, and also play
rackets with him.   In the one pursuit he throws cold
water on my genius, and in the other he makes blue
marks all over my body with a racket-ball; so that,
between the two, I shall not be sorry when our
connection terminates.   New Year's Eve was rather
slow.   However, J. King and myself, with Lightfoot,
who had by that time arrived, kept it in the most
solemn way with oysters in my room.   As the New
Year rang in from the peal of bells in the old clock-
tower opposite you may easily imagine the thoughts
which came crowding to the brain of each.   I con-
tented myself with wishing you a happy New Year
and all the good fortune attending thereupon.   J.
King saw rise in a long line before him all the ghosts
of the Joe Miller jokes which he had made during
the last twelve months; and Lightfoot silently composed the three verses of an appropriate hymn, which
he was with great difficulty prevented from reciting
on the spot.

"On the 6th, the Master found it necessary to retire
for change of air to the country, and insisted on our
leaving the college while he was away.   Jowett, who
was staying at Cowley in a little farmhouse, asked me
to go and stay with him.   It was dreadfully cold and
dreadfully windy, and only two very back bedrooms,

and one sitting-room, with a miserable fireplace. One might hear the wintry wind howling in the turrets and the pine-tops, had there been either turrets or pine trees within several miles, which, unfortunately, there were not. It was, however, very instructive to see the great Professor of Greek inventing more than Arian errors on the other side of the table. Having been able to discover, by a close contact with that remarkable individual, the chief *sine quâ nons* for a heretic, you may expect to see me coming out strong in that line. One is to hum very melancholy airs during breakfast; another is always to fill up the teapot before you have put in any tea; thirdly, to have no watch, and to lie asleep till twelve o'clock.

"I think with application I shall be able to master all these requisites except the last, which my regular habits completely prevent me from accomplishing. I go in every day to my coach. . . . The roads about Oxford are becoming dreadfully insecure. Garrotting is setting in with a virulence only equalled by the inclemency of the weather. Accordingly, as no one, in such a state of things, is safe, should you in the next three or four days see in any of the daily papers a paragraph headed 'Extraordinary Heroism!' I should advise you to read it. Besides reading the Ethics, I have been writing for the Latin verse; a poem which, though I say it who should not say it, is perhaps *the very finest* which, etc., etc."

No part of University life is more delightful than the reading-parties with which under-graduates, who are going in for honours, or otherwise bent on study, are accustomed to occupy a portion of the Long Vacation. Con-. genial companions, a common object, common tastes, freedom from every sort of restraint or disturbance, delightful rambles on some neigh-bouring moor or mountain-side—all tend to make the weeks flow gaily by. Nowhere does greater intimacy prevail, or intimacy ripen more quickly into friendship. Several of Charles Bowen's summers were thus employed. In 1858 he spent some weeks in Borrowdale with his friends Craig Sellar and Austen Leigh, " coaching" them for their final examination ; a labour of love, which, his pupils gratefully remembered, was performed with all the pains-taking assiduity which had characterized the preparation for his own degree. Another autumn we spent at Goslar, in the Hartz Mountains, and afterwards at Heidelberg ;

another at Portinscale, on the shores of Derwentwater; another at Aberfeldy; another in South Wales, at Bethgellert. On these occasions, unless I am deceived by the mirage which hangs over the scenery of forty years ago, Charles Bowen was seen in his most charming aspect. His gaiety of spirit broke out in every sort of fun; his sweetness of disposition threw a charm over the common details of daily existence. His brightness made it impossible to be dull. None of us, indeed, thought of dulness. Life lay open before us, fair with gracious promises. With boyish enthusiasm we read, we talked, we argued, we let speculation take a daring flight. Sometimes Newman, putting a finishing touch to the intellectual panoply with which he was presently to face the examiners, would recall us to a serious mood, and sober our too exuberant mirth with an historical disquisition. Sometimes Craig Sellar would give a foretaste of the meta-physical prowess which was to secure him a

First Class in the schools ; or Cordery, graceful
and accomplished scholar, conspicuous amongst
the first-fruits of the then recently opened
competitive system for the Indian Civil Service,
would exhibit the fine scholarship which subsequently graced his translation of the " Iliad."
Those of us who remember those days may be
forgiven for investing our recollection with some
of the romance which belongs to the days of
long ago. We seemed to be wandering through

> " Lands where not a leaf was dumb ;
> But all the lavish hills would hum
> The murmur of a happy Pan :

> " When each by turns was guide to each,
>   And Fancy light from Fancy caught ;
>   And thought leapt out to wed with thought,
> Ere thought could wed itself with speech.

> " And all we met was fair and good,
>   And all was good that Time could bring ;
>   And all the secret of the Spring
> Moved in the chambers of the blood.

> " And many an old philosophy
>   On Argive hills divinely sang ;
>   And round us all the thicket rang
> To many a flute of Arcady."

So sounds the far-off music of that pleasant retrospect, with some enchantment, perhaps, lent by distance, but still recalling a delightful time.

One of Charles Bowen's brother scholars— W. W. Merry, gayest and most mercurial of the sons of learning, whom forty years have sobered into a Public Orator and the Rector of a College—sends me a memento of their college days, and the learned pastimes with which the Balliol scholars of that day beguiled their leisure. " It was," he writes, "a joint attempt to translate Charles Kingsley's 'Sands of Dee' into something which should resemble a Virgilian eclogue. Bowen and I spent a fireside evening over it, when we were lodging at Mason's; and we were not highly critical. I think that the result pleased us."

THE SANDS OF DEE.

"' I, revoca pastas, revoca, Galatea, iuvencas :
I, Galatea, modo et (nox ingruit) ipsa redito.'
Surgebat madidis humescens flatibus Auster,
Auster, triste sonans et multa spumens unda.
Sola per incertas virgo incedebat arenas.

" I, revoca pastas, revoca, Galatea, iuvencas.
Interea lento repens allabitur æstu
Pontus, et occiduo pronus se littore fundit,
Includitque tegens late, atque intercipit unda.
Deinde vapor glomerat cæcoque volumine nubes,
Prospectum eripiens oculis : nec rursus ademptam
Cara domus notique lares videre puellam.

" I, revoca pastas, revoca, Galatea, iuvencas.
Nescio quid raris in summo marmore Devæ
Retibus interlucet, hiemps quod forte revulsum,
Summisit pelago, et palis infinit acutis
Mobile ; seu foret alga puellaresve capilli,
Nam neque tam pulcher nec tam spectabilis auro,
Deva, tuis unquam salmo se sustulit undis.

" I, revoca pastas, revoca, Galatea, iuvencas.
Illa quidem exigua nabat iam frigida cymba,
Triste onus, at multo sulcati remige fluctus
Ingluvie circum horrebant fremituque minaci.
Advexere pii tandem ad sua littora nautæ,
Littoreoque locant iuvenilia membra sepulcro.
Atque aliquis pastas etiamnum forte iuvencas
Audierit revocantem, et remo acclinis inanes
Excipit ad Devæ fatalia littora voces."

Charles Bowen's taste of classical versifica-
tion remained undiminished to the end of his
life. The art is no longer, I believe, held
in the high esteem which it enjoyed in the
days when it was regarded as the crowning

accomplishment of good scholarship. But Bowen found amusement and interest in it, and would often while away a leisure afternoon with his brother Edward, or some other congenial companion, in playing with the subtleties of a difficult translation. The following few specimens belong to quite his latest years. His friends will value them.

CROSSING THE BAR.

(TENNYSON.)

" Vesper adest, tandem nitet Hesperus ; in mare magnum
    Vox me cœlicolum, clarior ære, ciet.
Nulla tamen circa portum fremat unda reluctans,
    Funibus ut scissis in vada cæca feror.
Agmine me pleno fluctus trahat, absit amico
    Spuma salo, tacitas unda serenet aquas,
Dum pars immensi fueram qui marmoris olim
    Æquoreas repeto, quæ genuere, domos.

" Certa monent me signa, vocat lux ultima navim ;
    Imminet in vasto nox obeunda mari.
Digressu at nostro lacrimas compescite, amici ;
    Non ego deflendas cogor inire vias.
Namque licet rerum metas ac tempora linquens
    Vel procul hinc, fluctu me retrahente, vehar,
Præsentem inveniam, portuque egressus habebo
    Recturum cursus par freta vasta Deum."

"I STROVE WITH NONE."

(W. S. LANDOR.)

" I strove with none, for none was worthy strife ;
   Nature I loved, and, after nature, Art.
 I warmed both hands before the fire of life :
   It sinks, and I am ready to depart."

(C. S. C. B.)

" Non contra indignos ingloria bella petebam ;
   Semper erant silvæ, musaque noster amor.
 Hospes ut igne foci, vitâ sic largiter usus,
   Discedo, flammâ depereunte, libens."

REFRAIN.

(TENNYSON.)

" Mourning your losses, O Earth,
     Heart-weary and overdone?
 But all's well that ends well ;
     Arise and follow the sun."

" Quid gemis elapsos inconsolabilis annos
   Assiduo, Tellus, fessa labore nimis?
 Fit bene, supremam bene quod finitur ad horam ;
   Perfice volvendas, sole trahente, vices."

                                            1893.

A letter which Charles Bowen wrote to
Arthur Austen Leigh in 1857, from Goslar, gives
a pleasant idea of his way of life and mood at

this time. It is full of affectionate nicknames. His friend Bullock Hall is abbreviated into " Bull." Austen Leigh himself is " Dear Amyas."

" Herr Battenstadt, Goslar.
"Am Hartz, Hanover.

" DEAR AMYAS,

"Were it not for the intense heat of the weather, and the swarms of confounded flies that compel one to expend all one's extra indignation upon them, I should treat in the severest possible way your suggestion that I have been too lazy to write. The author of the present—to borrow for one brief moment the dignified style of some of our *best* letter-writers—has been up this morning at five o'clock, partly, I will confess it, owing to the aforesaid flies, partly from a strong sense of duty, which summoned him to Herodotus. From five to eight he read, took a crust of bread from eight to nine, and then till past two o'clock again employed himself in the study of history and of literature. All the shooting he does is with Dowe's Greek canon; all the riding or driving with his Aristotle cab. After this eloquent defence of one so deserving, I will now relate to you what has happened since I wrote to console you under your affliction. On arriving, with my usual punctuality, at the steamer at least one

G

hour and a half before the time, I found no Bull
on board, and left, surrounded by a multitude of Germans and of Jews, in the best of possible spirits, and,
I feel bound to add, all in the dirtiest possible shirts.
A marine debility which often attends sea-voyages,
coupled with the extreme simplicity of my foreign
vocabulary, prevented me from either converting the
Jews or conversing with the Germans. Add to this
that I was unable to get a berth, and that at the
last crisis I had left behind my railway-wrapper—a
new one—and my overcoat, and that it rained pretty
heavily for twenty-four hours, and you will have a
picture of my sufferings.

"Before arriving at Hamburg, our captain thought
it advisable to run us ashore in the Elbe. However,
at last we reached land safely, and I explored the town
under the safe conduct of an English clergyman,
whose acquaintance I had made upon the voyage.
Late in the evening of the day after, I found myself
in Goslar, where for five days I amused myself as
best I could in the society of the natives, with whom
my chief connecting-link was that we both spoke
languages that were branches of the great Aryan
family. On the first morning, to my horror, I discovered that I had managed to come in for the very
beginning of a festival which lasts eight days, called
the 'Free-shooters'—so named because they stand
in a plain and fire at a target in the distance, with
perfect indifference as to who happens to be walking

in the road between. In the evening the whole
population turn out to dance; and as my bedroom
was not very far off, I had quite sufficient. You will
naturally expect me to sketch in broad outline the
chief characteristics of the country and the natives.
The first thing, my dear Amyas, is that they are all
so like each other it is quite impossible to distinguish
between any of them; the second that, obviously
from motives of economy, their toilette is unaccom-
panied with any process like washing; the third is,
that they all shake hands with you, whether you
know them or not, and ask whether you remember
their name. The effort of memory requisite for the
latter feat is rendered less needful by the fact that, if
you did recollect it, it would be utterly impossible
to pronounce it. Bull, having been here last year,
is on terms of affection and intimacy with the whole
town, from the peer to the peasant. The clergyman
of the town, having been informed by him that I was
at Oxford, the next time we met, took the opportunity
of addressing me as Lieber Herr Doctor, evidently
completely taken in by my grave and reverential
demeanour during the German service, and the intelligent way in which I joined in the hymn. There is a
German young fellow who has just come here from
some Hussar regiment for his health, who talks
English in the most beautiful way, and who, I am
dreadfully afraid, is going to pay us a visit at Oxford
in the autumn, unless he should be, providentially,

shot in a duel which he has to fight first. Bull and
I are perfectly convinced he means to challenge us,
in which case I shall decline on the plea that I am
brought up for the Church. I need not say the very
affable manners of the Bull quite preclude the possibility of his being called out.

"There is a celebrated quack-doctor here who is
patronized by the King of Hanover. Crowds of
people flock here from Germany to him, and submit
to a six weeks' regimen for the benefit of their health.
When introduced to him, you are met by the startling
question whether you are quite sure you have not
got water on the chest, or a tendency towards
apoplexy ; and if you deny it, he immediately replies
that being ignorant of your disease is the very worst
symptom of the whole.

"Once a week we go a long expedition into the
country, which is really very beautiful. The other
days we go into the woods near, play at billiards,
drink coffee at the different places of resort, and in the
evening go up a neighbouring mountain called the
Catten-berg, to see the sun set, as a slight concession
to the sentimental disposition of Bullock. The little
dogs here are *much* nicer, and much *better-behaved*
and SUBMISSIVE, than the little dogs in England. We
have not yet been to the Brocken to see the spectre—
we are waiting for Cunningham ; besides, Bullock is
so intensely poetical that I am quite afraid to be with
him in the dark. Every morning at half-past five a

long train of cows and goats wind past our house, on their way up the mountains, and at about the same hour in the evening return, all with bells round their necks, making a noise which can be heard for miles. Three times a week we have a *gewitter*—that is, about four or five hours of thunder and lightning, accompanied with rain—after which the sky clears, and you are roasted alive till the next *gewitter*.

" My brother, with a thoughtfulness seldom seen in the younger brothers of great families, carefully selects, about once a week, the daily paper that contains least news in it—about ten columns of advertisements, and the gratifying telegraphic intelligence that the India mail is in sight off Trieste—and forwards it to us, postage studiously left unpaid ; so we have all the important dispatches never later than a month after you have them in England.

" The other day we were startled by the arrival of a policeman of the town, with two suspicious-looking bits of paper, which we at once conceived to be warrants of arrest for having assisted in putting out a gigantic fire about a night or two before, at which we laboured from eleven till four, to the intense amusement of the population, who stood round and watched. However, the two documents turned out to be permissions to live here, signed by the most despotic potentates of Goslar, and got up entirely regardless of expense. As we had not asked anybody's leave, or even thought of doing so, much less

signified our intention of residing here at all, we were
much gratified with the attention.   We inhabit a little
house (detached from a larger one), holding two bedrooms and a sitting-room, a kind of stone-floored
apartment where we have our baths, and a little
summer-house or arbour, where we take our meals.
When Cunningham comes, I shall relinquish him my
room, and migrate to the larger house, where resides
a Russian baron and his little boy of about eight
years old, who is, without exception, the most appal-
lingly polite little creature I ever saw, and insists on
always bowing repeatedly when you meet him."

During the Christmas Vacation of 1857
Charles Bowen stayed up at Oxford, having
allowed himself only a few days' holiday at his
home, which was now at Winchester.   On
December the 29th he writes to Austen Leigh,
giving him careful advice as to the selection
of a private tutor, and going on in a pleasant
vein of friendly banter.   " I had occasion the
other day," he adds in a postscript, "to think
of an observation, which is as follows : Why
is Arthur Austen Leigh rightly called a good
bat ?   Because a bat is a little creature, which

goes in very early in the morning, and does not come out till very late in the evening. Of course, this answer does not apply to those occasions on which I bowl on the opposite side."

Two days later he writes to Austen Leigh a bright, affectionate letter of good wishes for the incoming year.

"To-night being the last night of the old year, I am making preparations to see the new one in with intellectual conviviality, and shall, accordingly, read Thucydides till twelve o'clock, and, when the hour strikes, begin the Fifth Book of the Ethics; so 1858 has every reason to feel gratified. . . . Last New Year, I remember, Johnny King and I inaugurated together, and I have no doubt that, as he is away, I shall miss the air of accuracy and detail which he threw over the proceedings. I have every reason to believe that two ladies are occupying Sellar's rooms during his absence, and am thinking of sending for his cigars, lest they should use them all up. If they were widows, I should do so at once, as the connection between that portion of the fairer sex and weeds is too obvious to require explanation. Jowett is away, elaborating heresy in the vicinity of London.

Really, I don't at all dislike the solitude of Oxford, though I find difficulty in getting myself to go out regularly. . . . It is nine o'clock ; the Union is shutting up. Good-bye for the last time in 1857.

"Your very affectionate friend,

"C. B."

In the spring of the following year (1858) Bowen writes in high spirits from Eastbourne, where he and Sellar were making their first experiment in independent housekeeping.

"We wandered up and down looking for lodgings. In the course of our search Sellar suddenly developed the most wonderful arithmetical powers, hitherto, except in Smalls, entirely undeveloped. He beat down four lodginghouse-keepers in four successive quarters of an hour, leaving one delicate woman in tears and an infirm old lady in a paralytic fit. At last we got some, in a very nice house, and after Sellar had logically proved to the owner that she ought to be thankful to take us in for nothing, we came to terms. . . . We provide our own maintenance. This, as you might expect, is a rather terrible affair, and we have just had dinner upon the joint results of our wasted minds. By-the-by, I ought to say that we entered the house only five hours ago, and Sellar has already let his fire out twice, and I have let mine out once; so the landlady does not think much of us.

"Now, my dear Amyas, if you have any regard for your own health or our prosperity, you will take a ticket at once, and come and read with us. . . . If you don't immediately come, I don't know what is to become of us, as Sellar has all my money, and is managing the accounts. I am anxious to take them out of his hands, and put them into those of a steady little animal like yourself. Sellar sends his love, and you are to come and bring Jolly and a Latin dictionary."

The first plunge of the Oxford scholar into his new profession was not encountered without some natural shudders of dislike. The contrast between London life and the familiar pursuits and pleasant intercourse of the University was, no doubt, more striking than agreeable. The legal neophyte was depressed by his uncongenial surroundings.

"I well recollect," he said, addressing the Birmingham Law Students' Society in after-years (January 8, 1884), "the dreary days with which my own experience of the law began, in the chambers of a once famous Lincoln's Inn conveyancer; the gloom of a

London atmosphere without, the whitewashed misery
of the pupil's room within—both rendered more
emphatic by what appeared to us to be the hopeless
dinginess of the occupations of the inhabitants. There
stood all our dismal text-books in rows—the endless
Acts of Parliament, the cases and the authorities, the
piles of forms and of precedents—calculated to ex-
tinguish all desire of knowledge, even in the most
thirsty soul.   To use the language of the sacred text,
it seemed a barren and a dry land in which no water
was.   And, with all this, no adequate method of
study, no sound and intelligent principle upon which
to collect and to assort our information.   One felt
like Dante before he descended into the shades.   ‘In
the middle of the journey of our life,’ says the great
Italian poet, ‘I found myself in a dark wood, for the
straight way was lost.   How hard it is to say what
a wild and rough and stubborn wood it was! So
bitter is the thought thereof that death hardly can
be more bitter.’ ”

So deep was this impression that for years
after, as Bowen told one of his friends, he used
to make a *détour* in order to avoid passing
these chambers, so greatly did he detest the
very sight of them.

Charles Bowen, however little he liked the

surroundings of his new life, set himself vigorously to work. Some of his letters at this time sound as if his depression had soon given way to a more cheerful mood. Here is one to Craig Sellar, overflowing with high spirits.

". . . Since I wrote last, I have been tried in the fire of tribulation, only to emerge therefrom a brighter jewel. You may be aware that, before Christmas, I came to London, and took lodgings, to which I was attracted by the pleasant look of the young landlady. They were cheap, they were commodious, and they were aristocratic. To one who believes in blood, it could not go for nothing that my landlord was door-keeper in the House of Lords, which, you know, is next best to being doorkeeper in the House of the Lord, and may be considered (judging from the shady appearance of the species pew-opener) to be even more remunerative. Nor was this the only privilege. Underneath dwelt a French marchioness, whose race, my landlord told me, was of the noblest. For her sake, I may venture to express a hope that her antiquity of family came anywhere near her antiquity of years. And on the ground-floor resided a vendor of that noxious weed, the use of which, I am happy to say, is unknown in the social circles in which you and I have mixed. The consequence of this con-fluence of nobility was, as might be expected, a

commercial crisis. The marchioness stopped pay-
ment ; the tobacco-merchant made his bright home,
all on a sudden, in the setting sun. You, perhaps, have
never been brought into contact suddenly with a bailiff.
The first occasion of meeting one is apt to give you
a slight shock.   But the feeling soon blows over when
you have been in immediate communion, as I was,
for three days.   On the whole, my bailiff was not a bad
fellow ; he had a deathlike appearance about the face,
like our common friend X., and I have reason, from
various circumstances, to conjecture that he fed
extensively on onions ; otherwise he was not a bad
kind of creature.   He helped me down with my
boxes, and I emigrated from the scene of pecuniary
embarrassment to my present lodgings at an under-
taker's.   Hearses run from here to all parts of
London.   I myself am thinking of taking to the
mute line, which, if gloomy, is at least profitable.
The funeral service is performed at all hours of the
day, and you can be buried at a moment's notice.   A
reduction is made when taking a quantity.   Children
and schools half price.   No connection with the
house over the way, which is likewise an under-
taker's. . . ."

In April, Bowen entered the chambers of
Mr. Christie, one of the most distinguished
conveyancers of the day.

"Yesterday morning," he writes, April 21, "I wound up with Hawkins, and betook myself to Christie's, 2, Stone Buildings, Lincoln's Inn, where I am at present endeavouring, as far as possible, to disturb the peace of domestic circles throughout the country by making blunders in marriage settlements and creating irremediable flaws in titles. As yet I have not been allowed to do much harm, but hope to be permitted to do more as soon as I have learnt a little about it. We are a very intellectual circle at Christie's. Only two Senior Wranglers at present, but no doubt more are coming."

Here he found in his preceptor a companion that could unbend to other and more congenial themes than law. "When I was a half-hatched student at Lincoln's Inn," he told an audience, many years later, " I was the pupil of a distinguished conveyancer who loved works of fiction, and many a half-hour have I spent with him discussing Balzac, when his confidential clerk was under the impression that we were settling the draft of some marriage settlement. . . ."

A letter written in 1860 to one of his cousins,

wife of a country clergyman, touches amus-
ingly on the alarm which Jowett's arrival in the
neighbourhood might occasion in clerical circles,
and smooths the way for a kindlier welcome
than he might otherwise have received.

"A cloud is gathering over Cliveden, and, indeed,
has perhaps already broken. The great Oxford
heretic has gone down to stay there for a few weeks,
and the atmosphere is probably charged with un-
orthodoxy at this very moment. I need hardly say
that I allude to Mr. Jowett. I wonder whether you
will come across him. He is gone to read with two
younger Balliol men during the Easter Vacation. If
George, in the course of his sermon, casts his eye
upon a small, delicate face, belonging to a little figure,
with a high forehead and whitening hair, and the look
of a saint, he may be sure that he is preaching to the
arch-heretic whose throne is on the banks of the Isis.
I do very much hope that some fortunate accident
may bring him in your way. I am sure that, theology
apart, you would like him excessively; though he is
very silent and reserved, he is a man of such taste and
moral refinement, and I feel (as many other Balliol
men, scattered all over England, feel) that I owe
more to him than to any other man in the world."

In this year occurs the earliest indication of

any serious failure in health.   Bowen's doctors
were peremptory in insisting on a long and
complete holiday, and in the spring he set out
upon a tour in France and Italy.   In France
he had the honour of making acquaintance with
Montalembert, who accorded the brilliant young
Oxonian a kindly welcome.   In Italy, his
friendship with Saffi—illustrious exile, for whom
Oxford had created a special Chair—made the
traveller the object of general hospitality in
liberal circles.   The holiday soon effected the
desired result, and in the autumn Bowen was
again immersed in law.

"I am a reformed character," he writes to
Mr. Austen Leigh, in October, 1860; "I
have not smoked a pipe or a cigar for seven
weeks, rise early, and am reading law from six
to eight hours a day.   I write this in chambers
at six, having arrived here and not left my
chair since ten.   What do you say to that?"

On January 27, 1861, Charles Bowen was
called to the Bar.   He writes next day telling

Austen Leigh of the event, and referring to
the contest which had just taken place between
Mr. Max Müller and Mr. Monier Williams for
the Sanscrit Chair, which had, unfortunately,
been influenced more by the theological prepossessions of the electorate than by a strict
regard to the merits of the candidates.

"So Max Müller didn't get it. I have for ever
ruined my prospects at the Bar by not writing to
congratulate Mr. Monier Williams's brother, who is a
solicitor. But I really could not do it, though I have
no doubt you will jeer at what I consider a noble and
disinterested conscientiousness.

"N.B.—I was yesterday called to the Bar. I have
already begun to keep a register of all my best and
most brilliant remarks for the benefit of some future
author of the Lives of the English Chancellors."

A great change in Charles Bowen's circumstances was now impending—a change which
was to add greatly to the pleasures and
anxieties of existence. In February, 1861, he
became engaged to be married to Emily
Frances, eldest daughter of Mr. James

Meadows Rendel, the distinguished civil engineer. Never was there a happier or more devoted lover, or one whose delight in his good fortune overflowed with more spontaneous gaiety of heart among his friends. A letter of congratulation upon this event from Professor Jowett shows how strong a bond of affection, at this time, existed between tutor and pupil.

"February 10, 1861.

"I write a line to congratulate you and to assure you that I have the most sincere pleasure in anything that promises happiness to you. I should be the most ungrateful of human beings not to feel deeply your affection for me, which indeed I have never been able to account for on any other principle than Falstaff's, 'He has given me medicines to make him love me.' It has been a great pleasure and good to me in a life which of late years has not been quite happily circumstanced, though I do not mean to complain of it.

"When shall we give an entertainment in honour of the young lady? I think that it is all as well that she has not £100,000 a year, as she will keep tugging at your gown until you get briefs. I wonder whether

H

I shall live to see any of my old pupils a Chancellor
or Chief Justice?

    " Ever yours affectionately,

        " B. JOWETT."

  In October, 1861, Bowen joined the Western
Circuit, and began the traditional routine of
the young barrister's career.

  " I have just been on my first Sessions," he writes
to A. C. Sellar from Streatham—the residence of A.
M. Rendel, who was soon to become his brother-in-
law — "and have had ten little briefs, and a bad
abscess on it, which latter has confined me for some
time to an inn at Portsmouth. I have, however, at
last, managed to get back to a sofa in more civilized
regions, and bidden adieu to chambermaids and
waiters with considerable joy."

  The young barrister's anxieties as to professional success became, naturally, acuter when
a prospective wife was added to the topics
about which he had to be anxious. Charles
Bowen, always a hard worker, worked harder
than ever. Besides his legal studies, which
were pursued with more than average zeal, he

had been, since 1859, adding to his resources by constant contributions to the *Saturday Review*. This paper had been founded on the ruins of the *Morning Chronicle* by several leading members of its staff. Mr. A. J. Beresford Hope was principal proprietor, Mr. J. Douglas Cook the editor. Bowen's University reputation had naturally attracted the attention of its conductors on the look-out for brilliant recruits, and, along with several young Oxford contemporaries, he had come to form one of its regular contributors.

The paper had attracted attention by its ability, its audacity, its unsparing attacks, the strong drop of acid that flavoured its outspokenness. In controversy it was vigorous and not too polite. The "Superfine Review" was the sneer in which Thackeray, provoked by some supposed affront, expressed his view of its pretentious refinement. Other victims consoled themselves with denouncing it as "The Saturday Reviler." The paper, at any rate, was a force,

and no mean one, in the world of journalism.
The staff formed a group of men of real distinction: Sir H. Maine, G. S. Venables, Lord
Cranborne (Marquess of Salisbury), T. C.
Sandars, J. F. Stephen, Sir W. Harcourt,
Goldwin Smith, and Mr. T. Scott, a London
incumbent of strong High Church prepossessions, a copious vocabulary, and a reckless pen.
Though most of the influential writers were
pronounced Liberals in politics and theology,
the views of the chief proprietor, Mr. A. J.
Beresford Hope, tended strongly in the direction
of High Church Conservatism, and these views
were ably supported by more than one of the
most brilliant contributors.

The consequence was that there ran through
the paper a strong vein of Conservatism, which
occasionally bewildered its readers, and produced, before long, a schism in the staff.

For a time, Mr. J. D. Cook's tact, good
nature, and easy-going epicureanism prevented
the discordant elements from breaking into

open war. But the truce was of no long
duration. Two striking personages in the
Liberal ranks were at this time the objects of
attack by the champions of orthodox theology.
Jowett's influential position at the University,
his quiet but undisguisedly progressive tone,
frequently provoked his opponents to open war.
Arthur Stanley, charming all readers by a
delightful style, and challenging opposition by
courageous championship of unpopular causes,
was not likely to be ignored by polemical
writers, alarmed at inroads on accepted views.
The occurrence of such attacks in the columns
of the *Saturday Review* placed the Liberal
contributors, especially those who were bound
to Jowett and Stanley by the ties of personal
affection, in an awkward predicament. They
could not but recognize that their presence and
co-operation gave weight to attacks which,
appearing in less distinguished company, might
hardly have attracted attention, and that,
however little they sympathized with the

assailants, they incurred responsibility for whatever pain or injury the newspaper, of which they were the supporters, was capable of inflicting.

In 1861, an attack on Stanley in the *Saturday Review* brought the latent antagonism to a head. Charles Bowen, J. F. Stephen, and others of the contributors seceded. Some efforts were made to start a rival journal, which should be exempt from such backslidings. Its editorship was offered, it would appear from one of Charles Bowen's letters, both to himself and Sir H. Maine. Both, however, had the wisdom to decline a dangerous and laborious post, which would have practically involved the abandonment of their profession.

The quarrel was ultimately adjusted by an arrangement which the seceding contributors considered as satisfactorily safeguarding them from any participation in such attacks for the future. Some letters on the subject, which passed between Charles Bowen and his friends, especially Professor Jowett and Stanley, throw an interesting light upon the dispute.

"You may be sure," Charles Bowen, in one of these, writes to Jowett, "that I never will write for any paper in which it is possible that either you or Stanley should be attacked, either directly or indirectly, by innuendo or otherwise. So that, if I go back to the *Saturday Review* (which I have not yet determined to do) it will be in case I should feel that there is no chance or possibility of a repetition of such articles as these last."

Here is a letter of Jowett's to Charles Bowen on the same subject.

"Stanley tells me that he wrote to urge you to continue your connection with the *Saturday Review*. I am sure I should wish you to do so, as far as I am concerned, but it did not occur to me to say this to you. And, depend upon it, it is really wiser to remain and try to influence the *Review*, and not allow —— to be its presiding genius. I am truly grateful and sensible of the strong proof of affection you showed to me, but I should not be at all the less so if you went back to it again, and I hope you will not be deterred by any considerations of this sort."

In another letter Jowett gives some excellent

counsel as to the spirit in which the project of a new journal should be carried out.

"I hear with much interest that some adventurous spirits are thinking of starting a new weekly review. Is this so? I hope you will have the best editor who can be found (no one occurs to me better than Sandars). It will be foolish in such a venture not to be liberal in the salary and in the payments to contributors.

"It is easy to see what such a review should not be; it should not be 'young and curly;' it should not inaugurate a new moral world; it should not carry on a warfare with the old *Saturday;* it should not begin with a flourish of trumpets, or announcement of principles, but creep into notice by the ability of its articles.

"It should be Liberal in politics, yet with the aim of making liberality palatable to the educated and aristocratic; it should be liberal in religion (not in the sense of the *Westminster*); it should have a distinct object (like the *Edinburgh* in old days) which would, in fact, be the politics of five or ten years hence. It should attach itself to some leading politicians, Lord John, Gladstone, Sir G. Lewis, Lord Stanley.

"It should not fanatically abuse the Emperor Napoleon or John Bright, or competitive examinations, or the Evangelical clergy. It should include

High Churchmen, and make religion one of its leading topics; it should have no 'isms,' no pretensions of superhuman virtue. Above all, it should be amusing.

"Stanley takes a view of the subject which is worth considering before you start, viz. that, after all, the amalgamation of opposites in the *Saturday* is more good than harm. But I think you might still continue to unite them in the new review.

"The real reconcilement of classes in the world and of parties in the Church; the balance of foreign and English interests in Europe; the working out and application of political economy to the interests of the lower classes, are fields in which a new review might hope to do some service. These sorts of aims look pompous when written down in this way; to do any good with them they should be concealed though pursued. Foolish aspirations and self-consciousness are, perhaps, the worst fault of taste a newspaper can have."

Of his own view of the controversy Bowen wrote to his friend, Craig Sellar, in a somewhat less measured strain than was habitual to him.

"Talking of 'Essays and Reviews,' why on earth is the Defence Fund not to publish the names of its contributors? It is perfectly contemptible, a lot of

skulking creatures believing in their hearts that the
men are all right, and yet leaving them alone to bear
the brunt of the fight, and getting themselves under
cover.   As for the conduct of all the semi-liberals on
the subject, it is simply damnable.   Half have stood
by in the dark stabbing their own side, and the others
have stood by and let them be stabbed.   Semi-
liberalism, by which I mean that dry polish of
literary refinement which innate Tories put on and
call it Liberalism, is getting so common that the
Conservatives can have everything their own way.
'Essays and Reviews' are not, I suppose, the tip-top
work of all the genius of the century; but they are
much better, on the whole, than the twaddle talked
on the other side.   I dare say you will think my
language altered since I left (for I have left) the
Saturday Review; and I do say the line the *Saturday Review* has taken about it has been dastardly in
the extreme."

In January, 1862, the marriage took place—
a courageous step for a man who had still his
professional position to secure, and all the
more courageous, in the Bowens' case, from
the circumstance that neither husband nor wife
were as robust in health as the struggle of a
barrister's life renders essential.   Charles

Bowen was probably in far more delicate health than he imagined. He was, in fact, in one important respect, an invalid. The process which ultimately cut short his life had, we must believe, already begun; the strain upon body and mind had been too severe. The games and enjoyments of school and college, though in one sense a refreshment, may, at the same time, have contributed to general exhaustion. He was now starting on a career which makes large calls on a man's physical and intellectual powers of endurance; which involves intense and protracted exertion; long days of watchfulness and concentration; short nights, or no nights; work done at the highest possible pressure, and, above all, done at racing pace; and he was doing this without any reserve of health and strength on which, in times of emergency, he might draw. The remainder of Charles Bowen's life was, accordingly, to a large extent, one long struggle against the breakdown which was ever close

at hand.   Only one result could be anticipated,
and that result ensued.

Those who had the opportunity of watching
him closely for the next few years, knew too
well how severe the struggle was, how
constant the interruptions from failing powers,
how serious the drain upon vital power.   His
temperament and training alike conduced to
exhaustion.

It is sometimes urged as a complaint against
University education that it tends to produce
a superfine article, too subtle, too exquisite,
too highly strung for the commonplace purposes of human life.   These highly wrought
machines, it is suggested, actually lose power
in practical business from their very finish and
perfection.   They do each piece of work
exquisitely—more exquisitely than the occasion
requires or deserves ; and this superfluous
excellence is achieved at enormous cost of
nerve and brain power.   The fires burn bright
and intense, but are apt too soon to burn

themselves out. There is the waste, which, as the proverb tells us, results, when razors of fine temper are used to cut blocks, or thoroughbred horses are put into sand-carts.

Many of such men, conscious of their unfitness for the rude business of life, and shrinking from contact with it, let their opportunities go by, and never emerge from obscurity. Others, more courageous and more ambitious, plunge boldly into the conflict, "breast the blows of circumstance," command the success which they deserve, and achieve celebrity. None the less the original impress remains. Such men are, at heart, philosophers and poets. Their quality shows itself in two directions. On the one hand, there is a certain exquisiteness of taste, a fastidiousness of judgment, a scrupulous nicety which nothing, falling short of the highest and most uncompromising standard of excellence, will satisfy; and which makes all work a painful and exhausting struggle after unattainable perfection. On the other hand, there is a counter influence, the sadness of insight, a besetting scepticism as to the interest and worth of human things; a haunting suspicion that the struggles, excitements, and prizes of existence are not worth the effort which they involve, that human achievement is but a troublesome illusion, and that, when all has been said and done, our little life is rounded with a sleep.

Some traces of such a habit of mind are, I think, observable throughout each part of Charles Bowen's career. His standard was so high that it cost a life-struggle to attain it. He attained it, or was nearer to doing so than most of his fellow-men. But the effort was too great. It undermined his constitution. It cost him his health, his life. To the end he was working with too fine an instrument, and it was shattered in the using. On the other hand, he never quite believed in life. Under a superficial gaiety there ran a vein of melancholy. Successes and honours rained thick upon him.

Under each lay the besetting suspicion that all is vanity.

Charles Bowen had been but a few months married when symptoms of delicacy began to reveal themselves. He suffered from repeated attacks of fever, the origin of which, when it could not be traced to malaria, had to be found in overstrain of powers and consequent nervous prostration. His nerves were in a condition of such morbid sensibility that the slightest noise or movement in the room where he was at work gave him acute distress. Nothing but a complete and prolonged rest, the doctors pronounced, would avail for the restoration of his health. But how unwelcome a prescription for the rising barrister! Charles Bowen refused to leave his work, and struggled on for two years more, when further resistance became impossible, and he was forced to acknowledge a complete breakdown.

It was decided that he should take a year's holiday. He went abroad with his wife, travelled leisurely along the Riviera, and passed the winter of 1865 and the following spring at Rome.   On their homeward journey the Bowens spent some weeks in Switzerland. They were joined by Mr. Bullock Hall at Seelisberg.   " There," says Mr. Hall, " we spent several delightful weeks, wandering in the woods, bathing in an upland lake near the Nicier Baum Rock.   Charles Bowen's health gradually re-established itself.   Towards the end of our stay he was able to join me in an eight-hour walk from Engelsberg, over the Surenen Pass to Altdorf."

The travellers returned to England in July. In the autumn Charles Bowen made a tour with Mr. Archibald Milman and myself in Norway.   Bowen and I started together from Hull.   One interest of the voyage to us was to test a specific for sea-sickness just then in vogue, viz. a long bag of ice applied to the spine.   As the passage was a rough one, our steamer a roller of the first order, and Bowen

a wretched sailor, the supposed prophylactic
had an excellent opportunity of making its
merits known. The result was disappointing,
and we arrived at Christiansund in a somewhat
prostrate condition. Bowen, however, found
material for fun in this and every other mishap
of our journey—then a much rougher business
than it has since become. We purchased
carrioles, and drove across to Dronheim,
stopping, as occasion offered, to walk, shoot, or
fish. At many of our stopping-places the
resources of our hosts did not go beyond beds
and hot water, and we depended on the tinned
provisions, which we carried with us, and our
own somewhat rudimentary cookery. One fact
was, I remember, borne in upon me, viz. that
a brilliant University scholar may be a very
indifferent hand at opening tins, or poaching
eggs. Now and again we unshipped the
wheels of our carrioles, and explored the silent
shores of lake or fiord. Our long drives were,
perforce, to a large extent, solitary, and it was,

I

doubtless, during some of these that Bowen's mood found utterance in the lines which, under the title, " Norway," he subsequently preserved in the little volume of " Verses by the Wayside." They form the best journal of his tour.

NORWAY.

" Down the still fiords, bay after shining bay,
    We sailed under the hills, beneath whose breast
Sleeps the great sea inviolate alway,
    Mountain-caressed.

" On either hand of us rose solitude,
    Filling the sky with summits. Each vast height,
Snow-capped, cloud-mantled, like a giant stood,
    Silent and infinite.

" Yet were not all things silent—there were cries
    Of more than mortal anguish and distress,
The sad wind, grieving down a precipice
    Into a wilderness

" Of ruined pines—and stormy water-rills,
    Flashing with foam, which since the sun first shone,
Have thundered down unheeded, and shall still
    Thunder unheeded on.

" And moans of 'wildered birds, and the great beat
    Of the wanning and the lapping of the sea,
Like a cold lover wailing at the feet
    Of one as cold as he.

" Sometimes a dusky porpoise slowly wheeled
    Sunwards in the mid channel ; from his lair
Sometimes an eagle, royally revealed,
    Swam down the fields of air.

" And underneath us, windless and serene,
    The ocean forest lay,
Long fairy drifts of rainbow woodland scene,
    Drowned in the purple bay ;

" Fair realms of fern, more exquisite than ours,
    More delicate and bright,
And endless glades of glimmering seaweed bowers,
    In golden water light.

" On such an afternoon to such a place
    Came sad Undine, and from some mountain shelf,
With desolate eyes and melancholy grace,
    A shadow of herself,

" Beheld in trance her youth return, the same
    As when, one summer morn, a sister band—
Knowledge and Love and Grief—together came,
    And took her by the hand.

" She felt white arms that waved, or seemed to wave,
    And, waving, call her downwards to the deep,
Where all her friendly waters, cold and grave,
    Lay mourning in their sleep,

" And sighed and rose, and turned her steps again
    Along the rock-hewn ledge, where, far aloof,
The sunset reddened on a lonely pane
    And a deserted roof."

We returned in October, to find a goodly
heap of letters, written throughout the tour,
waiting at the port of embarkation, to travel
homeward in our company.   Bowen could not
face the Skager Rack again, and preferred a
long land journey by Denmark.   He was
certainly much improved in health, and was
able to resume his professional work, though
still handicapped by occasional illnesses and
shattered nerves.   He had now a further
object for professional success.   He was a
father.   The eldest son, William, was born in
November, 1862 ; the second, Maxwell, in
October, 1865.

In 1868 public attention was occupied by
the dispute between the United States and
England as to the responsibilities of the latter
power for the injuries inflicted by the *Alabama*
on American shipping, after her escape from
an English port where she had been built.
The quarrel had lingered on for years, and had
only become the more acute from ineffectual

attempts at adjustment. English opinion—
strongly tinctured, in some classes, with
sympathy with the Southern States' struggle
for independence—was not prepared to admit
itself in the wrong. The United States, on
the other hand, deeply aggrieved at the
attitude of England, and naturally exasperated
at the losses inflicted by the *Alabama*, had
not the slightest intention of allowing the claim
to lapse for want of prosecution. The controversy had drifted to a critical stage. Mr.
Seward's offer to submit the case to arbitration,
at first declined by Lord Russell, had been
accepted in principle by Lord Stanley, but
subject to conditions with which the American
Government felt unable to comply. Lord
Stanley insisted that the arbitration should
proceed on the assumption that, at the date
of the Queen's Proclamation, May 13, 1861,
recognizing the Confederate States as a
belligerent power, a state of war did actually
exist, and that the question for the arbiter

should be whether, on this assumption, there had been any such failure on the part of Great Britain in its duties, as a neutral, towards the United States as to involve a moral responsibility to make good any losses arising there-from to American citizens. The Government of the United States, on the other hand, had throughout contended that the Queen's Proclamation was unjustifiable, and now insisted that this question, as well as that of subsequent negligence on the part of Great Britain, in her duties as a neutral, should be made part of the reference. Charles Bowen had formed a decided opinion on the subject, and formulated his opinions in a pamphlet, which was at once accepted, on both sides, as a learned, logical, and weighty statement of the case. His main object was to induce his countrymen to see the reasonableness of the United States' contention that the whole case should be submitted to arbitration. He believed that, on the question as to the existence of a state of

war at the date of the Queen's Proclamation,
the English Government were in the right;
none the less, he urged, Mr. Seward's position
was an intelligible one, and in any case
England's true policy would be to accept
the arbitration on Mr. Seward's conditions.
England had something to regret and to
repair in the matter of the *Alabama*, and it
did not become us "to approach in too
technical a spirit the terms of arbitration propounded by a nation which has suffered heavily
by our inadvertence." For the purpose of his
argument he had to controvert the doctrine
propounded by the well-known "Historicus,"
that a neutral nation is bound by no rule of
international law to enforce her own neutrality,
but is entitled, without ceasing to be a neutral,
to remit or assert, as it pleases, its neutral
rights in favour of one belligerent. Bowen
had little difficulty in demonstrating that this
contention was unsustainable, and was, in fact,
repudiated in the clearest terms, by the very

writers on whom " Historicus " relied. His exposition of this part of the case is an excellent
example of the qualities which, in after-years,
rendered his judgments admired models of all
that a judicial utterance should be. Every
point, however minute, is considered with
scrupulous nicety ; on the other hand, there
is a constant tendency to rise above details,
and to carry the argument into the higher and
clearer atmosphere of first principles. The
author's account, for instance, of the growth
of that somewhat vague and nebulous entity
known as "international law," stripped the
subject of much of its ambiguity, and cleared
the ground for that and any subsequent controversy in which international rights and
duties are in dispute. It is no longer the
mere lawyer who speaks, but the philosophic
historian, quickened with the lawyer's acumen.

Another branch of Bowen's argument was to
show that the circumstances of the *Alabama's*
escape were such as to raise a strong *primâ*

facie case of negligence against the British authorities, a contention which, at the present day, few would be found to dispute, but which, at the time, it required some courage to maintain against the strong prepossessions of English opinion. In claiming indemnity for such negligence before the arbitrator, the United States might, the author went on to urge, reasonably claim to show surrounding facts indicative of the general intention of the offending party. The Queen's Proclamation, hasty, premature, and contrary to the international law as Americans regarded it, was essentially such a fact. It showed *animus*, and went to favour the inference that England had not done her best to prevent the escape. Though not alleged as a ground of damages, it was, Americans might urge, an unfriendly and ungenerous step. And the friendliness or unfriendliness of our behaviour, from the summer of 1861 downwards, might be material to the question whether, in the summer of 1862, we dealt with the *Alabama* in a spirit of scrupulous neutrality. "The *animus* displayed in the one year might illustrate or support the argument of negligence in the next."

Another ground of C. Bowen's argument in favour of submitting the whole case to arbitration, rested on the consideration that it was impolitic for England to stand out as the champion of the extreme rights of neutrals, a doctrine which might be inconveniently enforced against herself in case of a naval war. Regard, too, must be had to the desirability of terminating a dangerous estrangement between England and the United States. In adopting the basis of arbitration in cases where her own interests were concerned, England would be taking one step further towards a higher level of civilization.

"Universal peace, sung of by poets, scoffed at by cynics, dreamed of by good men, is still hidden far beyond our sight, in the cloudland of the future; but if we cannot hope to reach it, we may, at least, desire to move towards it. The Congress of Paris, which closed the Crimean War, recognized the value of the humane principle of arbitration—put forward in the first instance by England's envoys—and recommended it to Europe. It may be hoped that we are not going to move backwards by all these years. For every reason, for the sake of right and justice, as well as for the sake of English interests, it is to be desired that the protracted controversy should soon end."

The pamphlet excited great interest.

"On my way from the House last night," writes Mr. T. Hughes, "I called at Lady Stanley's, where I found Lord Russell sitting. He had read your pamphlet, and was very much struck by its ability and fairness. You will be pleased to hear this. For myself, it seems to me as near perfection as possible, and if it does not decide the question in the right sense, nothing will. It will, at any rate, furnish us all with weapons for the debate next month."

Another congratulatory letter comes from Professor Jowett, followed, unhappily, too soon by another of condolence and encouragement in the illness which followed the publication of the pamphlet.

"I am very much grieved," Jowett writes, "to hear

about your illness.   I hope that you will not lose
heart, and then all will be well.   Unless you break
down in health altogether, I am confident of your
success.   And if you do break down, which I don't
anticipate, I am sure that you may have another sort
of success in a distinguished literary life.

"Therefore θάρρει, ὦ βέλτιστε, and don't think much
of the loss of three weeks or a month as a piece taken
out of life.   There is plenty of time to recover that."

"The pamphlet is talked about and makes its
way," Jowett writes later.   "It came out at the right
time, and is not thought, in the present temper of
people's minds, to be un-English.   There is a greater
sense of change of opinion going on in England
now than I ever remember.   They don't know what
to think about Ireland, about the Church, about
classical education ; and anybody who would make
a row might get something done."

The illness proved more serious than Jowett
had anticipated.   C. Bowen was for three
months confined to his bed, or sofa.   He
underwent a severe operation, suffered greatly,
and made but a slow recovery.

A letter written early in this year, by Charles
Bowen to his cousin, Miss Frances Steel Graves,
is of interest, as being conceived in a more

serious vein than was habitual to him in his communications with others, and giving an insight into the graver side of his character. It is the wise and sympathetic utterance of a high-minded man to one whose esteem and sympathy he valued, and for whose well-being he felt a warm concern.

Speaking of religious opinions, he writes—

"It is difficult to explain the position of any one person about these things; it generally stands by itself; and at the present day most men who have ever thought seriously on such matters are, perhaps, in a very puzzling position, especially as regards the freedom with which they ought to discuss or proclaim their opinions to those whom they care for. I think myself that the right course is, never (within certain limits, which I need not now explain) to pretend distinctly to think what one does not, but, if necessary, to avoid all controversy. For the rest, a sincere wish to learn what is true, however much it may conflict with any of one's cherished ideas, and a resolution, at all costs, to follow what seems to one (after hearing as much of all sides as one can) to be true, is to my mind the one thing to be aimed at in life. I am sure that it is no easy task; it frequently involves pain to others and pain to one's self; often, as in the case of

some people whose course I daily am observing, it
involves the sacrifice of all social and worldly ambition
and success.   I think that, if people, who are hurt and
grieved by finding those they care for following any
path of thought they dislike, would reflect on it, they
would see that loyalty to the cause of what one
soberly (after weighing all sides, to the best of one's
judgment) believes to represent truth, is the first
thing needful.   What I wish for myself is more
fearlessness in holding to what I in my heart think,
than encouragement to disguise from myself what I
do think.   If I was only as brave as some I know,
and long have known, I should be far more what I
should like.   Not that I feel or value less, dear
Frances, your New Year's wish.   I feel it very deeply ;
and my New Year's wish for you is in return, that
you may have as happy and noble a life as I think
you will have, being kept as far as may be from all
moods and phases of theological discussion or enquiry,
which are unnecessary ; but, with this, that you may
never, in the course of time, drift into a worldly way
of forgetting that life is too short for the world's ways
or opinions or distinctions to be of much consequence
to any one, and that the true heroes of life are often
to be found among those on whose fearless advocacy
of what they believe the world is making social war.
I am not one of such people myself, and don't profess
to be, but I know some of them ; and would rather
be amongst them than amongst their critics.   I say

this, because I neither should like you to go on mis-
understanding my views about theology, philosophy,
and politics, as I see that you have been paining
yourself, in an affectionate way, over them ; and
because I would rather you understood from myself
the reason why I abstain from professing before you
to like to discuss such subjects.   I am glad to have
got your letter, and shall always keep it among my
most valued papers.

"Good-bye, and believe me, ever your very affectionate cousin, dear Frances, and your faithful friend,

"CHARLES BOWEN."

Bowen's early years at the Bar were not
without their anxieties and disappointments.
His reputation for ability was established, but
the question had yet to be solved whether his
ability was of that precise order which would
command success at the Bar.   His extreme
youthfulness of appearance, his academic refinement, his polished satire, his apologetic manner,
his deference to the opinions of others, his lack
of the comfortable air of self-assertion which
so largely commands the suffrages of mankind,
stood, no doubt, in the way of his early success.

Solicitors are a sceptical race, not easily impressed by University distinctions.   Bowen
was not, at the outset, a fluent or commanding
speaker, and the points which he was naturally
inclined to take were often too fine and too
subtle for the audience or the occasion.   Even
in high quarters he did not immediately find
favour.   Chief Justice Cockburn, on Bowen's
first appearance before him, listened at the
outset with interest and attention ; but, as the
argument proceeded, is said to have thrown
himself back in his chair with a gesture of
impatience and disappointment.   Still less
were the common juries of the Western
Circuit likely to appreciate the delicate irony
of a Platonic orator.   " If you consider, gentle-
men," Bowen is reported to have said, in
prosecuting a marauder, who was caught on
the roof of a house with the implements of his
trade in hand, "that the accused was on the
roof of the house for the purpose of enjoying
the midnight breeze, and, by pure accident,

happened to have about him the necessary tools of a housebreaker, with no dishonest intention of employing them, you will, of course, acquit him"—a recommendation which the jury proceeded to carry out by a verdict of acquittal.

Bowen's first appearance at Westminster before the Court in Banc was a somewhat trying ordeal to a junior's nerves. The argument turned on an alleged misdirection by Chief Baron Pollock. The Chief Baron himself presided in the appellate tribunal, and had a clear recollection of what his charge had been. Bowen's remembrance was equally distinct, and he had shorthand notes and other corroborative evidence at his back. The Chief Baron grew more and more positive; positiveness presently kindled into wrath. Bowen, resolved on death or victory, was pertinacious, insistent, unabashed. Prometheus defying the Olympians was scarcely playing a more audacious *rôle* than this neophyte in the profession essaying to convince the Chief

K

Baron, against his will, as to the language he had used. The wrath was becoming very Olympian indeed, and the consequences threatened to be serious, when a friendly missive from a member of the Court—Sir George Honeyman, if I remember rightly—warned the young combatant that there are bounds to human temerity, and occasions on which the assault should not be pressed too far, and that the Chief Baron's health would be imperilled by a prolongation of the encounter. I remember, as we walked homeward from Westminster that evening—both of us in great excitement at the events of the afternoon, Bowen certain of his cause, but doubtful as to his prudence and his skill—how we reassured ourselves by the reflection that Chief Barons, after all, were mortals like ourselves, must have once worn the stuff gown and sighed for briefs, and would probably have a latent sympathy for an advocate too zealous to be easily abashed.

Bowen's first case of importance was an arbitration case in which Fitzjames Stephen and he were engaged on behalf of the firm of Nettlefold and Chamberlain, of which Mr. (the Right Honourable) Joseph Chamberlain was then a member. The question was one concerning patent rights, and involved much technical detail as to intricate machinery and an investigation of very elaborate accounts. It was deferred for several months in order to give time for Bowen's recovery to be sufficiently complete to allow him to take an active part in it. Mr. Chamberlain formed a lasting friendship with both the counsel in the case.

Charles Bowen's abilities were now rapidly forcing their way to recognition. In 1868 he was appointed a member of the Totnes Bribery Commission. It was found, however, that his standing at the Bar disqualified him for the post. The difficulty had to be got over by his appointment as Secretary to the

Commission.   In 1869 he was made a Revising Barrister.   In the winter of the following year he was made a member of the Truck Commission, and was appointed Recorder of Penzance, an office which, before long, the increase of his professional work rendered it necessary for him to resign.

In November of this year (1869) the birth of another child—Ethel, now Mrs. Wedgwood—added another item to the list of life's pleasures and anxieties.   The necessity of success was more than ever imperative.

In 1871 the Tichborne Claimant began to figure in the courts.   This celebrated case occupied so important a place in Charles Bowen's early professional career, and involved such serious results to his health, that it may be interesting to recall the outline of the two great trials to which it gave rise, to explain the inordinate length to which the proceedings were protracted, and to show the excessive demands which, from their special character, they made on the powers, physical and mental, of the counsel engaged.

The proceedings began in an ejectment suit in Chancery on the part of the Claimant for the purpose of asserting his claim to the Tichborne Estate, as heir of Sir John Tichborne, Bart., who died in 1862. It next came before the Court of Common Pleas in the shape of an issue, directed by the Court of Chancery, as to whether the plaintiff was, or was not, heir to Sir John Tichborne. The trial of this issue began in June, 1871, and speedily attracted public attention, partly from the strange and romantic character of the plaintiff's story, partly from exertions of the plaintiff and his supporters to obtain notoriety. It was obvious from the outset that the inquiry would be a protracted one. The plaintiff's task would have daunted all but a sort of bulldog audacity, strongly reinforced by impudence. His case rested on improbabilities so gross that it seems strange that any one could have given it a moment's

credence.   An explanation had to be given of
Sir Roger Tichborne's incomprehensible silence
from the date of his disappearance after the
foundering of the *Bella*, in 1854, to his produc-
tion by his Australian *entrepreneurs* in 1865,
and of the strange metamorphosis which, on the
assumption of identity, had befallen him in
physiognomy, style, habits, recollections, tastes,
language, education—in short, every physical,
mental, and moral characteristic.

This huge fabric of lies had to be pieced
together as it could best be with every scrap
of evidence which could be collected for the
purpose.   Some of this was supplied by accom-
plices, who gave the plaintiff information as to
the real Sir Roger Tichborne's earlier career,
and so enabled him to impose on the credulity of
other witnesses, who thereupon convinced themselves that they recognized in a coarse and obese
ruffian the features of the slight, half-French
gentleman of their recollections.   The main
case for the defence assumed a twofold aspect,

one negative, viz. that the plaintiff was not
Sir Roger Tichborne, the other positive, viz.
that he was Arthur Orton, the son of a Wapping
butcher. The case broke out, as it proceeded,
into numerous ramifications, each of which
extended almost indefinitely the area of the
inquiry. For instance, one of the plaintiff's
answers, like most of them, a reckless jump in
the dark, involved a brutal imputation on the
character of an honourable and spotless lady,
which it became necessary to refute. At a late
stage of the proceedings it became necessary
to send a commission to Australia to test the
truthfulness of the story of the alleged rescue
of Roger Tichborne after the foundering of the
Bella. It was the business of the counsel for the
defendant to test at every point the soundness
of the entire fabric of the plaintiff's story, to
follow out every clue, to bring to light every in-
consistency. For this purpose the smallest facts
were as important as the biggest. If a contradiction could be shown between the details, it did

not matter, for the purpose in hand, how minute
these details were.   There was not, probably, in
the entire mass of the evidence a single fact
which, except for the purposes of the trial, it would
have been worth while for any human being
to remember for five minutes.   But for the
purposes of the trial it was essential that every
fact should be remembered with equal exactness, and should be in readiness to be produced
at a moment's notice for the corroboration or
contradiction of some other item of the story.
When it is remembered that the plaintiff's case
occupied many weeks in the telling, and many
months in being pulled to pieces, it is easy to
appreciate how enormous a strain it must have
imposed on those whose business it was to
remember, arrange, and co-ordinate the various
pieces of this elaborately tesselated work, and
to appreciate the ultimate result as to the truth
or falsity of the whole.   It was necessarily a
prolonged operation.   The plaintiff's cross-
examination, for instance, lasted for twenty-two

days. After the Long Vacation of 1871, the case was resumed in November. The examination and cross-examination of the witness Baigent, a connection of the family, son of a drawing-master at Winchester, who professed himself satisfied of the Claimant's identity, and had been active in promoting his claim, lasted for thirteen days. It was not till the seventieth day of the hearing that Sergeant Ballantine concluded the plaintiff's case. The sittings were resumed on the 15th of January, 1872, the Attorney-General's opening speech for the defendant lasting for a month. The absurdity of the claim became too patent to justify further investigation, and on the 4th of March the jury intimated that they did not stand in need of further evidence for the purpose of arriving at their verdict. After a few days' deliberation, Sergeant Ballantine, on the plaintiff's behalf, elected to be non-suited.

Thus, after lasting for a year, the plaintiff's claim collapsed. There remained the grave

question of his criminal liability for the fiction
which he had ventured to bring into court.
The Court directed a prosecution for perjury,
and on April 9, 1872, the Grand Jury found
a true bill against the Claimant on an indictment for perjury, first, on his affidavits in
Chancery, and next for his statements in the
Court of Common Pleas. The trial was fixed
for November. On November 23rd, the
Attorney-General claimed to have a trial at
Bar, a trial, that is, by jury with two or more
judges sitting in bench—a form of proceed-
ing provided by the English law for criminal
trials of especial importance. In April, 1873,
the trial commenced, before Chief Justice
Cockburn and Justices Mellor and Lush.
Hawkins, Q.C. (now Mr. Justice Hawkins),
Sergeant Parry, Chapman Barber of the Equity
Bar, J. C. (now Mr. Justice) Mathew, and
Bowen were counsel for the prosecution. The
counsel for the defence were Kenealy, Q.C.,
and MacMahon. The Claimant was charged

with perjury in the proceedings in Chancery and in the civil action : (1) in asserting that he was Sir Roger Tichborne ; and (2) in denying that he was Arthur Orton.

Mr. Hawkins, in his opening speech, traced Roger Tichborne's career, his life at home and at Stoneyhurst; his attachment to his cousin ; his departure for America; his arrival at Valparaiso in June, 1853 ; the sailing of the *Bella* from Rio, bound for New York, on her last fatal voyage in April, 1854 ; and, making good use of the ample material afforded by the Attorney-General's protracted cross-examination in the civil case, he called attention to the innumerable mistakes and lapses of memory into which the Claimant had been betrayed.

On the 21st of July, 1873, Dr. Kenealy began to open the case for the defence. His speech lasted till August 21st. The case for the accused was closed on October 27th. The trial was then adjourned in order to give time for the prosecution to secure evidence from

South America and Australia, to meet a certain
portion of the defendant's story which had
come to light only in the later stages of the
case.

On December 2nd, Dr. Kenealy began to
sum up the evidence for the defence. He was
still speaking when the year 1873 came to an
end. He concluded on January 14, 1874, and
the next day Hawkins, Q.C., began his reply
upon the whole case. Popular feeling had now
begun to run high in favour of the Claimant, and
Mr. Hawkins and Sergeant Parry had, on one
occasion, to be protected by the police against
the violence of a mob. Mr. Hawkins's reply
was not concluded till January 28, 1874, and
the following day Chief Justice began his sum-
ming up of the case. His charge to the jury
lasted for eighteen sittings, and the keen
interest with which the case was followed by
the public may be gathered from the fact that
the report of the charge in the *Times* occupied
no less than one hundred and eighty columns of

that paper.   On February 28th the case closed, having lasted through one hundred and eighty-eight sittings.   The jury found the accused guilty, and Mellor, J., pronounced a sentence of seven years' imprisonment on each count of the indictment.

Thus, from the middle of 1871 till the end of February, 1874, the burthen of this great case was weighing upon Bowen's mind.   He devoted to it the whole of his powers, intellectual and physical.   His familiarity with every fact in it was complete.   He used to say that he did not believe that there was a single fact in the evidence of which he was not fully cognizant, and of which he was not prepared on the spur of the moment to give an immediate and correct account—a preparedness which his leader frequently put to the test.   During the civil action it became an open secret that the Attorney-General depended largely on his junior's acumen and industry. The mental strain was tremendous.   The previous preparation

of the case, the consideration of how the
evidence, given each day through weeks and
months of examination and cross-examination,
affected the rest of the story.   The long hours
—day after day, of unremitting attention in the .
oppressive atmosphere of a crowded court—
three years of work done at the highest possible level of excellence, and frequently at
moments when physical ill health made all exertion dangerous—all this, no doubt, seriously
undermined Bowen's constitution, and did his
health irreparable injury.

Hard-worked as the junior counsel were,
they found leisure to poke a little good-natured
fun at one another, and to relieve the tedium
of the trial by an occasional outburst of
frivolity.   The   following   Wordsworthian
narration is a skit of Charles Bowen's at
the loss of fees which his friend J. C.
Mathew was supposed to be sustaining
through his absorption in the Tichborne
Trial.

OLD MATHEW.

" Amid the case that never ends,
    We sat and held a brief,
Mathew and I—a pair of friends,
    And one a withered leaf.

" ' And, Mathew,' said I, ' let us talk,
    Amidst this noisy scene,
Of the old days in King's Bench Walk,
    When you and I were green.'

" ' My friend,' said Mathew, ' all is done—
    A withered leaf am I ;
Last Guildhall sittings there were none
    Left so completely dry.

" ' The serjeant in Red Lion Square
    A modest pittance gleans ;
Hawkins and Barber do not care,
    For they have ample means.

" ' But I, since first this case began,
    Sit here for ever chained ;
No one consults me, and by none
    Am I enough retained.

" ' My faithful clerk and I are short
    Of cash ; he now foresees
A sad old age—some County Court
    Far from the Common Pleas.'

" ' And if Guildhall be lost to you,
    Dear Mathew, that will be,
Since Johnny Gray is just and true,
    Considered in the fee.

"'And, Mathew, on yon Bench,' I cried,
  'Thou yet shalt sit as chief.'
To this he gloomily replied,
  'I am a withered leaf.'

"Meanwhile, about us and afar,
  Again arose the storm :
Kenealy and the Chief at war,
  Each in the best of form.

"Of virtue, science, letters, truth,
  They talked till all was blue ;
Of Paul de Kock, the bane of youth,
  Of Banfield Moore Carew.

"If fools are oftener fat or thin ;
  Which first forget their tongue ;
Why all tobacco, mixed with gin,
  Is poison to the young.

"And whether Fielding's better bred,
  Or Sterne—so full of fun ;
Poor Mathew sighed and shook his head,
  'The Will of God be done.'"

The following supposed address by the
Claimant, a "Baronet of the British Kingdom,"
to the leading Counsel for the Prosecution, also
from Charles Bowen's pen, recalls pleasantly
some of the humours of the trial.

LINES ADDRESSED TO MR. HAWKINS, Q.C., BY A. B. OF B. K.

"Though what you say of pore old Braine,
    Hawk'ns, have give me serous pain,
    Yet well she know, and i the same,
    Them as instructs you is to blame.
    So, 'Awkins, if the crowd is cross
    And anchor round to seise your hoss,
    If Wicher cannot set you free,
    Come in my Broom, and drive with me.

"I quite agree with what you say,
    'Awkins, in Court the other day,
    That pore Kenealy's sad disgrace
    Ought not to pregudice my case ;
    Bogle and i has always thought
    He ain't a fought it as he ought ;
    Why aggravate the Court and you,
    When it's not nersessary to?

"I lick the way you sets to work ;
    Your highly paid, but does not shirk.
    See how old Onslow catch it hot
    About that pictur of the grot.
    O, 'Awkins, had i had but you !
    You knows what's what—and does it too.
    Onslow and Whalley both may be——
    'Awkins, you come and dine with me."

In 1872 Bowen was appointed, on Sir John
Coleridge's nomination, Junior Standing Counsel

to the Treasury, professionally known as
" Attorney-General's Devil," a post of much
labour and responsibility, and regarded as a
certain road to further professional achievement.   Sir John Coleridge recognized the
services which his junior had rendered to
him in the Tichborne case, and on other
occasions, with generous and affectionate
enthusiasm.

"Will you," he writes in March, 1872, "put the
volumes I send herewith amongst your books for my
sake.   I am in some degree responsible for their
publication, and they are dedicated to me.   The copy
is a large paper one, so it has at least the merit of
rarity.   But nothing I can give you can ever repay
my debt to you, not only in this case (in which I
desire to record the simple truth that you are the
main author of the success we have had), but for
many years past, during which you have been in all
ways of unspeakable service to me, and during which
my love and regard for you has deepened and
strengthened day by day till it has become part of
my nature, and can end only with my life.
                "Your grateful and affectionate   ı
                    "J. D. COLERIDGE."

Writing to Mrs. Bowen in April, 1872, he says—

"I am very sorry Charlie does not get on faster; at the same time, considering the strain upon him, and the *superhuman* work he did for so long, and with such anxious feeling, I am half inclined to wonder sometimes he is no worse. Please God he will soon come round again. I am sure if I had worked half as hard as he did, or had cared as he did, I should have been dead long ago. Get him to be lazy and cold hearted, and you can't think how well he will be."

From 1872 forward till his appointment to a Judgeship in 1879, Charles Bowen was immersed in his profession. He appeared on behalf of the Government in all important common-law and commercial cases, and his reputation was now so high as to render it an object with litigants to secure his services for cases in which individual interests were concerned. Some of these attracted much public attention, as, for instance, the prolonged inquiry into the Competence of the Arches Court of Canterbury to suspend Mr. Mackonochie *ab officio et bene-ficio*, the trial of Mr. Wilson for his views on the Inspiration of Scripture, and that of Mr. Voysey on a similar topic. His argument in Julius *v*. The Bishop of Oxford was the last, and perhaps the most brilliant, of his achievements at the Bar.

Of Bowen's method in the practice of his profession an interesting account is given by Mr. H. H. Cunynghame, now Under-Secretary at the Home Office, who was at one time—as also was Mr. Asquith—a pupil in Lord Bowen's chambers.

"Of all his characteristics perhaps none was more striking than the extraordinary pains he took over his work. His pleadings and opinions were revised again and again, and I believe that, if he had had a draft submitted to him every day of his life, he would have altered it every day in some particular. This habit was due not only to the conscientious and anxious care he bestowed on whatever he did, but also to the acuteness of his critical judgment, which never could tolerate the smallest fault or even imperfection.

"To this thoroughness, as well as to the extra-ordinary subtlety of his intellect, he owed, I think, his success in those days. When I first joined his chambers, he recommended me to read Blackstone in the original edition, without the wholesale changes which have so marred the symmetry of that work. This recommendation was in pursuance of his favourite maxim, to rely on general principles in law, and take, as he used to express it, a bird's-eye view of a legal subject.

"Connected with this almost abnormal development of the critical faculty was his distrust of himself. He used, I really believe, to torment himself, even after his success was assured, with fears that he would find his chambers deserted, and get no more briefs. Every case he did, however trivial, absorbed his whole attention, and I am convinced that he often impaired his efforts in great cases, by the fatigue induced by his attention to small ones. 'Cases,' he said, 'are won at chambers;' and the pains he took, and the ingenuity he displayed in the preliminary steps of a case are inconceivable.

"It is difficult to decide whether or no he was an orator. If by an orator is meant one who can amuse or convince an intellectual audience, then few men had greater oratorical gifts. His keen sense of humour and taste for satire came out, not merely at the private dinner-table, but also on more public occasions. In court he was rarely very successful

with juries, on account of the great difficulty he felt
in letting his mind run on the same line with theirs,
or in understanding the views and mode of reasoning
of an ordinary juryman. But in court or at chambers,
where the extraordinary originality of his reasoning
found scope, he compelled attention, and his good
humour, always ready on the slightest encouragement
to break out into fun, lightened the heaviest proceedings.

"During a part of his career he certainly overworked
his brain, but this I suppose is the inevitable fate of
barristers of pre-eminent ability and of a highly and
nervously organized temperament. But through all
his work, his kindness of heart never flagged. He
shrank, almost to a fault, from giving pain, and I am
by no means sure that it would not often have been
better for his pupils if we had had a sterner and even
rougher master. ,

"Although no one would have placed Lord Bowen
among the class of popular orators, it must by no
means be thought he was incapable of making a good
address on ordinary occasions. His addresses at the
opening of the Truck Commission, and of the
Featherstone Commission, are both models of a firm,
judicious, and conciliatory style.

"Those who knew him, believed that he had qualities
far greater than those of a mere lawyer, and that, if
his life had been spared, he would have played a part
in the wider arena, to which he was called when he

was made a peer, not less interesting and original than that which he played as a barrister and judge."

In 1875 the Bowens determined to have a country home, to which they might send their children, and whither they might themselves repair in the holiday intervals of London life. They had, in 1872, purchased a cottage on Slaugham Common with this object, and they were now determined to migrate to Colwood, a pretty Sussex village between Cookfield and Horsham, the scenery and quietness of which were greatly to the taste of both. Here much of their leisure time for the rest of Charles Bowen's life was spent. The change from London to a perfectly country scene was the best of medicaments for an overworked body and brain. In 1881 they partially rebuilt the house, on a scale better suited to the requirements of later life, and Lady Bowen's taste and care embellished it with lovely woodland. The plan was congenial to them both. Its

agreeableness was enhanced by the circumstance of their much-esteemed friends, the
Dean of Westminster and Mrs. Bradley,
choosing a country retreat in the same neighbourhood, an arrangement which allowed of
a renewal of the intimacy of old Rugby days.

"During all last year," C. Bowen wrote to a friend
in 1882, " my wife and I were building at our country
house or cottage in Sussex—Colwood. We came to
the conclusion that the air was so fine, and suited so
well my wife and the children, that it would be a pity
to leave it. Accordingly at Colwood we settled.
Last year we spent in building ; this in catching cold
in the rooms recently built ; next year in furnishing
and papering them ; the year after in paying our bills
—the order in which everybody proceeds who occupies
a new house. This year, or the second of the series,
we have spent our summer holidays at Colwood.
Before doing so I went to Scotland to yacht, and in
passing saw the Sellars. Do you remember Ardtornish,
where you came to the conclusion that H. had a very
frivolous set of friends ? There it was, this summer,
just the same, and Mrs. Sellar waving her hand-
kerchief out of the window to the Sound of Mull."

Bowen's busy professional life at the Bar

and on the Bench left but little leisure or opportunity for speaking on non-professional subjects. Nor did his genius play at ease in its natural element at the commonplace level of after-dinner oratory. On a congenial occasion, however, he could speak with brilliancy and effect. At Oxford, for instance, in the hall of his old college and in the company of his old companions, he was at his very best. In 1877 a great festival was held at Balliol on the occasion of the opening of the new hall: Bowen was called upon at a very late period of the festivities to propose the master's health. Such a theme inspired him. Writing of this, Sir M. E. Grant Duff says—

"In January, 1877, I saw him obtain a real triumph. It was at the opening of the new hall of Balliol. The Master presided, and spoke admirably, so did the Archbishop of Canterbury, Dean Stanley, Coleridge, and several others. It was the very best after-dinner speaking to which I ever listened, but there was a great deal of it ; and when Bowen rose in the body of the room to make the last speech, somewhere about midnight, he had, assuredly, no easy task. So

well, however, did he play his part that, in a very few
moments, the jaded audience was laughing with him,
and felt, when he ended, that the gathering had
received from him the final touch which made it
perfect."

At this dinner Bowen returned thanks,
on behalf of the fellows and scholars of the
college, for a toast proposed in their honour.
The speech abounds in characteristic touches
of seriousness, sentiment, and wit.

"I well remember the first time in my life that I
ever received a letter from a great man. I had gone
back to school, fresh from the fever of a Balliol
examination, and two days later one whose distinguished literary genius, whose fearless courage,
and generous devotion to his friends have made his
name a household word throughout the land, wrote
to congratulate an unknown schoolboy on having
been elected to a Balliol scholarship. It would be
impossible to forget the words in which he described
his own pride and pleasure in former times at having
been elected a Balliol scholar, or how he dwelt on the
golden opportunity afforded to those who are fortunate
enough to join so noble a company. And it was a
strange chance when I found on entering this room—

for the master of Balliol, with the forgetfulness of
genius, had omitted to tell me that I had to make a
speech to-night—it was a strange chance by which I
have found myself chosen in the name of the Fellows
and Scholars of the present and the past to acknowledge a toast given in their honour by the writer of
my first letter from a great man. Is there any one
in this hall who believes it to be an easy task to
stand here and speak in the name of the Fellows and
Scholars of Balliol past and present? I will not
allude to the historic past, on which the Dean of
Westminster has dwelt. I prefer to speak of the
Fellows of Balliol as my contemporaries, and as I
knew them when we entered on our Oxford course.
There was Jowett, the first tutor of the college, to
whom, at the risk of offending his delicacy, I cannot
refrain on an occasion such as this from openly
acknowledging the deep debt of gratitude I and
many others must always owe him. There was
Woolcomb, the most courteous of Oxford tutors;
Walrond, the modern Hercules, whose choice was
always the choice of virtue; Lonsdale, absent in
body to-night, but never absent from the recollection
of those who experienced his kindness. There was
Palmer, the best of friends; Riddell, whose life was
all that is beautiful and good, the Sir Galahad of
Oxford; Henry Smith, greater than Janus, whose
gates face three ways: towards classics, mathematics,
and philosophy. And next to the Fellows there

were the Scholars. The memories of great names
had descended to us at the Scholars' Table. Matthew
Arnold, the shy student of the Thames, who has
always been of the company of the poets; Lord
Coleridge, the worthy inheritor of a name dear to
Oxford; Grant, the lucid interpreter of the greatest
of ancient philosophers of whom I was once a barren
pupil. Holden and Hornby and Bradley, Freemantle,
and Henry Oxenham, the glory of the Oxford
Union, rivalled only by my friend George Brodrick.
I cannot say with what delight I have found myself
placed here between two brother-members, more
distinguished than myself, of my old boat behind
whom I rowed when, under the guidance of Walter
Morrison for the last time in many years, Balliol was
head of the river. I recollect a famous passage in
Chateaubriand where he describes his feelings on
revisiting Venice in later life. He had seen her in
his youth, and he saw her again when he was old.
In one sense she was still the same Venice, still St.
Mark's with its cupolas and its piazzas, still the
Rialto, still the blue lagoons—and yet it was no
longer the old Venice. Something in its glory had
departed, and, reflecting on the loss, at last he came
sadly to the conclusion that the wind which blows
upon an older head blows no longer from a happy
shore. The associations of travel fade; but the
associations of our school and our University never
alter. Venice may change, but Oxford and Balliol

are still the same ; and standing here to-night, I
desire to express our deep recognition of the fortune
that has enabled us to assemble once more within
the shadows of our college walls, to refresh ourselves
here in memory, the only fountain of perpetual youth,
and once again, if only for an evening, to dream that
we are young."

In the autumn of 1878 Charles Bowen's
health broke down too completely to allow
of any attempt to struggle on without a break.
It was obvious that nothing but a complete
change of life and scene would suffice to restore
him.   He started, accordingly, on a protracted
tour.   He went, in the first instance, to Stockholm, and thence travelled on to St. Petersburg,
Moscow, Kiev, and ultimately, Constantinople.
His letters to his wife from each place give
detailed and picturesque accounts of his experiences ; but they were intended for a wife's
eye alone, and it is better not to quote them.
There is perceptible throughout a painful tone
of exhaustion.   He was evidently so prostrate
with fatigue that the question of getting through

the light labours of his tour was sometimes oppressive.

In the following year an opportunity of relief presented itself. On the retirement of Mr. Justice Mellor from the Bench, a Judgeship was offered to Charles Bowen. After some hesitation and misgivings, he determined to accept it. The decision was, in some senses, a death-blow to his hopes—his dreams of ambition. It closed the door finally on the possibility of a Parliamentary career. It forced him to acknowledge to himself—what he was always anxious to ignore—that health must be a dominant factor in his scheme of life, and that his failing physical powers made a continuance of the sort of life he had led for some years past impossible. The change, though it brought a welcome and salutary close to intellectual toil for which Bowen's strength had become wholly inadequate, was not without its drawbacks. The transition from the excitement of advocacy, and from the participation in a succession of important and interesting cases to the uneventful tranquillity of the Bench, produced a painful reaction; Bowen had not been in a great practice long enough to lose a zest for it. He quitted it with regret, and with a sense of a tyrannous necessity, which over-rode his fondest wishes; and he came to his new duties, unfortunately, without any such interval of rest as would have restored his enfeebled powers, and enabled him to start on the new chapter of his career with cheerfulness and satisfaction. He sank into great depression of spirits. As the first sensation of relief passed away, the surrender of ambitious hopes left a sense of disappointment. Nor were the duties of his new post sufficiently congenial to reconcile him to the change. The functions of a Judge, sitting at Nisi Prius, are not of the character for which Charles Bowen's faculties and temperament were especially suited. His mind was too rare, too subtle, too conscious of nice

distinctions and refinements to make it easy
for him to range himself on a level with the
average Common Jury, and put an argument
in the way which they would find most lucid
and convincing.   It is probable that both
Judge and Jury were conscious of the wide
interval which separated them.

In the autumn of 1880 he took a house
at Llantysilio, near Llangollen, in North Wales,
in the hope that the change of scene and air
might be beneficial ; but the experiment was
not altogether successful.   Bowen's habitual
gaiety was overclouded ; his general condition
remained unsatisfactory, his health wavering
and uncertain ; he was restless and melancholy.
The friends who visited him in Wales were
painfully impressed with the feeling that something was amiss.   In the late autumn, when on
a visit to his brother-in-law, Mr. Stewart (now
Lord) Rendel, he had a very serious attack of
illness.   As to this Jowett writes, October 16,
1880, a letter of encouragement.

"I am very sorry," he says, "to hear that you are unwell, though, to say the truth, I am not very much surprised at it. For I thought, when I was with you, that you had a great load of overwork from which to recover, and you must expect during the next two years a good deal of oscillation of mind and nerves before you can regain a firm or settled state.

"I hope that you will be very quiet and sleepy, and discharge your mind of care and anxiety. This sort of philosophy or religion is a discipline which I think that we can impress upon ourselves. You have in all probability thirty years of life before you, and can very well spare two of them for the recovery of health."

In one sense the change of life was altogether welcome. It promised the opportunity of renewing friendships for which the stress of professional work had left hardly any leisure. In replying to his old friend, the Warden of Merton, who had written to congratulate him on his appointment, Charles Bowen dwells on this pleasant prospect.

"I have always had to thank you for so much and such generous friendship that another piece of thanks

M

does not add much to my obligation, though your letter added greatly to my pleasure.

"I do not seriously believe that many men could have gone through the physical fatigue I have for nearly ten years. I know *you* could not have done it ; and, if a Judgeship comes at the end of it, I don't say that the honour is less appreciable ; but the price paid has been heavy.

"I do delight to think that I shall get back to my old friends, I hope, after my long exile, and that, of all, you and I will meet much oftener, and live more together.

"Thank you so much. I am now, as always,

"Your grateful and affectionate friend,

"C. B."

With reference to his appointment to a Judgeship, Bowen writes to his old friend J. C., now Mr. Justice Mathew, a graceful letter, veiling under playfulness the desire to apologize to a competitor, whom for the moment he was leaving behind him in the race. The first paragraph refers to the religious parties which a late Lord Chancellor was in the habit of giving, and which, so ran the joke, aspiring barristers attended with a view to professional advancement.

"MY DEAR J. C.,

"Thanks for your kind letter. My religious character, I believe, was what ultimately brought the Judgeship down. Perhaps you are not aware *where* or *how* I spent last Sunday.

"Did you observe I had disappeared?

"Where was I?

"Echo pauses for a reply. I am afraid I am beginning to mix my metaphors, so I (like echo) pause.

"My dear J. C., *I* know, and the profession knows, that you are twenty times as fit to be a Judge as anybody at the Bar; and I can only feel what an advantage it is to be the A.-G.'s devil.

"I am always

"Yours faithfully,

"CHARLES BOWEN."

In June, 1888, Charles Bowen was appointed, in succession to Lord Justice Holker, a member of the Court of Appeal. Here he found himself in a congenial sphere, and engaged in the sort of work for which his intellectual constitution and previous training had pre-eminently qualified him.

"It is upon his work there," * says Lord Davey,

* *Law Quarterly Review*, July, 1894.

" that his judicial reputation will rest. Law, to
Bowen, was not a mere collection of rules, but was
the embodiment of the conscience of the nation. He
recognized the duty of endeavouring to apply legal
doctrines so as to meet, in his own words, the
broadening requirements of a growing country and
gradual illumination of the public conscience. He
was, therefore, the master, and not the servant, of his
knowledge. It might seem exaggerated if one said
that he combined the breadth of Lord Mansfield
with the accuracy of Lord Wensleydale ; but it would
give an idea of the truth. Lord Bowen will be remembered among the great judges who steered
the ship in the transition from the old system to
the new."

It was natural that a temperament and intellect of this order should feel but scanty regard
for legal technicalities in comparison with the
intrinsic merits of the case. A famous English
Judge is reported to have observed complacently
that a plaintiff, who had been ruined by suing
in trespass, might have succeeded if he had
sued on the case, but that if trespass and case
ever came to be confounded, there would be an
end of English jurisprudence. Bowen's view

of the value of legal formalities was the very opposite of this.

"Indeed," says Lord Davey, "a Judge of his clearness of vision and accurate habits of thought could safely dispense with the aid of pleadings. Lord Bowen, in his anxiety that justice should be done, was indulgent—some of his colleagues thought, over-indulgent—to slips of practice and mistakes. He would never let a client suffer, if he could help it, from the ignorance or carelessness of his advisers, or even his own obstinacy. One who sat with him for many years speaks of the extent to which he would 'let a blundering or obstinate litigant turn round and restate his case, or get his case tried, or do whatever he wanted.' 'It arose,' he said, 'from his great fear lest the litigant should not, in the end, get whatever was his right in the beginning.' 'It may be asserted,' says Bowen, in 1887, 'without fear of contradiction, that it is not possible in the year 1887 for an honest client in the Supreme Court to be defeated by any mere technicality, by any mistaken step in his litigation.' Some readers will, perhaps, think this boast a little rose-coloured."

It is, at any rate, the boast of a mind wholly free from that subservience to technicalities which has cramped so many otherwise fine

judicial intellects, and has at times made the
procedure of English Courts more like some
intricate and bewildering game than a con-
trivance for finding out the truth and adminis-
tering justice.

Lord Justice Fry, one of the most intimate
of C. Bowen's friends on the Bench, and a
colleague who probably saw more of his work
from day to day than any other, has summed up
his estimate of his judicial character in the
following appreciative sketch, which, with his
permission, I transfer from the article in which
it first appeared.

"What impressed me almost most of all about him
was his intense sense of duty in the discharge of his
office. Both intellectually and morally he was keenly
sensitive to anything which appeared to him like the
enunciation of bad law, or still more to anything like
the slightest miscarriage of justice. Either of these
things seemed to inflict a personal—almost a physical
—wound on him : and the pains which he took both
to do his own part in the administration of justice to
the very best of his great abilities, and so far as he
could to secure the very best working of the machinery

of the law, were infinite.   He never wearied of
investigating or discussing a point so long as he
thought that anything remained to be got at—or
that there was any hope of bringing about an agree-
ment of opinion amongst colleagues who were inclin-
ing to differ : and anything like a suggestion to him
that he was worrying himself more than was necessary
he always gravely put aside.   I doubt whether those
who listened to or read his brilliant judgments would
have the least notion of how much thought and
persistent effort he had given to them : and the
extreme rapidity of his intellectual operations made
this all the more remarkable to those who by daily
intercourse saw 'the very pulse of the machine.'   If
Bowen had any personal ambition, it was entirely
subordinated by him to the sense of duty to which I
have referred—so completely that I do not believe
that it was an efficient principle to any extent in
his actions or his thoughts.   Furthermore, I do not
believe that he had any vanity.   It is a very common
characteristic of men of great abilities ; but I never
detected a trace of it in him."

Lord Justice Fry has been good enough to
supplement the foregoing summary by a more
detailed description.

"When Bowen became a Judge of the Court of
Queen's Bench, a friendship began between us and

our families; and after I followed him, by about a year, into the Court of Appeal, my intercourse with him was constant. We often sat in the same Court, and for years may almost be said to have worked shoulder to shoulder. In the last note I had from him he described himself as a horse who had lost his stable-companion (by my retirement from the Bench).

"In the moral qualities which befit a Judge he was, I think, perfect. I have already endeavoured to express in a passage which you know what most struck me about him in that respect ; nor do I know that I can add much to it.

"Intellectually his very excellencies were, to some extent, defects, and they were his only defects. The rapidity and subtlety of his mind were so greatly in excess of these qualities in most men, and even of most able men, that they sometimes produced want of harmony in the positions of his mind and of those of the others, whether Judges or Counsel, who were engaged in the discussion ; and sometimes his most brilliant judgments were, I believe, hardly appreciated by those who heard them. The rapidity of his mental operations, the suddenness with which he grasped the facts and arguments of a case, were surprising. If, as of course sometimes happened, he had made some omission or error in his apprehension of the case, he was equally rapid in his appreciation of the least suggestion of his error, and in the rearrangement of the whole

subject in his mind. It was just the same in a game;
he saw, as it were intuitively, the whole position of
the board and the relations of the pieces; and I have
heard it said that if he were present on any occasion,
when some speech or event caused general amusement, a distinct interval of time could be perceived
between the first ripples from Bowen and the general
roar of laughter. The result of this great rapidity
was that the advocate, opening a case, was often
outrun by his hearer; and that, whilst he was laying
the foundations of his argument, Bowen was engaged
in the critical examination of the details of the
ornaments of the top story. So, too, with regard to
the subtlety of his mind. Details, distinctions, which
seemed to most minds subtle, refined, microscopic,
appeared, I believe, to his mental eye to stand out
broad and clear as the strong features of the matter.
What seemed molecular to most minds seemed
massive to him; and this was not without its drawbacks in a world where law is concerned with the
common affairs of common men; and I believe that
it made him less successful in addressing juries both
from the Bar and from the Bench than many men of
lesser intellects.

"He held the highest possible views of the duties
of the judicial office, and he was very jealous of the
independence of the individual Judge; very unwilling
to lay down or allow the laying down of any rules of
practice which should fetter the discretion or limit

the power or responsibility of each man in the
discharge of that high office.

"It is impossible to think of Bowen in connection
with the Bench without recalling some of those
delightfully humorous accounts which he sometimes
gave of his sufferings there. One speech at a Middle
Temple dinner, in which he described his labours in
the search after 'an equity,' and illustrated it by a
story about Confucius and his disciples, must, I think,
survive in the memory of most of his hearers.

"Bowen was not incapable of just anger. No man
of a high and noble nature, such as his, could possibly
be so; and he was acutely wounded by anything
which he thought to be deliberate unkindness towards
himself or others. But of sharpness or unkindness
he was as incapable as of stupidity; and I can hardly
recall that I ever heard an impatient word from his
lips upon the Bench.

"To me the recollection of the days in which he
and I worked together in the duties of our office—
lightened as they were to me by his constant kindness,
as well as by the aid of his great powers—will ever
remain one of the brightest of my life. But even to
the casual observer it must have been apparent
that he

> 'Hath borne his faculties so meek, hath been
> So clear in his great office,'

that his loss to the country is no ordinary one."

Another of his colleagues, Mr. Justice
Mathew, whose friendship dated from the
days when they were both wandering in the
cold shades of brieflessness, bears a similar
testimony.

" My acquaintance with Bowen," he writes, "began
after his call. He had been ill, and had returned to
work somewhat anxious and despondent. Coleridge,
who was an early friend, and had a great admiration
for him, cheered him with an offer to share his
chambers. This helped to make him known, and
Coleridge, who was most faithful to those he liked,
was constant and confident in predictions, the speedy
fulfilment of which he was enabled in some measure
to secure.

" Bowen's first appearance in Court was not successful. He was most graciously received in the Queen's
Bench by Cockburn, who had heard of him. Many
of us, as Juniors, had learned 'to trace the day's
disasters in the morning face' of the C. J.; but he
beamed upon Bowen. Alas! a weak voice and a
delivery hesitating and somewhat over-refined for
the rough and rapid work of the Bar, annoyed the
great man, and he ceased to listen. Bowen had to
bear the disappointment, with which most of us have
started ; but the incident did not occur again. Those

who succeed and those who don't, as a general rule,
fail only once.

"We became intimate friends. He soon got into
business, and we were often opposed to each other.
He was strenuous and adroit in controversy, but
he was always considerate, and never forgot that
his adversary was a comrade and a learned friend.
Through his whole career at the Bar and on the
Bench he remained the same. Time had not hurt
him. He was always kindly, bright, and youthful,
ready to discuss any subject, literary, political, or
professional. Even when he chose to be frivolous he
could be intellectual ; and his peculiar humour played
about and brightened all he said. He was altogether
free from affectation, and never was there a mind
clearer of cant. With a certain dignity that the
consciousness of his power gave him, he was never
dictatorial or self-important ; and he could listen,
sometimes under trying circumstances, without the
slightest appearance of effort. Commonplace people
enjoyed his society as much as those of his own
scholarly kind. His courtesy made them for the
time his equals.

"While he was at the Bar, and, afterwards, on the
Bench, he was in the habit of discussing with great
eagerness the cases that came before him. He called
in a friend, less to assist him with advice than to
arbitrate between the conflicting views, which were
presented by him with extraordinary subtlety and

minuteness. He explored every corner and cranny of the evidence, and turned over every small fact with unwearied curiosity, lest anything should escape him which might afford a clue to the right conclusion. He was not often wrong.

"He was sensitive to a fault, as are so many of the highly trained Oxford men—as, notably, was Newman. A strong opinion in confident language ruffled him; an incautious phrase wounded him; a slight uneasiness of manner, or a short interval of silence, showed that something had gone wrong, and had to be set right. He was as sensitive for others as for himself, and I have more than once heard him offer a prolonged and embarrassing explanation, to some solemn colleague or grave divine, of something he had said that he thought might not have been liked.

"His humour was his own, and was most difficult of description. Something sparkling and original might always be counted upon. His manner never foreshadowed the good thing coming. His melancholy air diverted all suspicion. But a certain cheerful gleam of his eye, and a kindly smile that hovered about his lips, rescued many an excellent jest from the peril of being overlooked.

"He was the most loyal and generous of friends. Looking back over many years, I have known few upon whom Heaven conferred so much genius, so benevolent a disposition, and so manly a character.

In his fidelity to all the charities of life, great and small, there never was a better Christian.

"He was strongly Liberal in his opinions, and the profession is largely indebted to him for reforms in the law, and for a better system of legal education. Many of the Resolutions of the Judges on the subject of procedure were prepared by him ; and his colleagues were much influenced by his advice in the proposal for the creation of a Court for the revision of sentences—a reform not likely to be carried in these timid times, but with the necessity for which he was profoundly impressed."

One other testimony from a brother Judge may here be added—that of the Master of the Rolls, pronounced on the morning after Lord Bowen's death, in the Court of Appeal, where so large a portion of his judicial career had been passed.

"He was," Lord Esher said, "one of the most admirable Judges who has sat on the Bench in my time. His knowledge of the whole law was so perfect, and was so entirely at his command, that I myself have no doubt that he had studied every proposition of law minutely, accurately, and carefully, in order to learn it, long before he was called upon to bring it into practice. His knowledge was so complete that it is almost beyond my powers of expression. His reasoning was so extremely accurate and so beautifully fine that what he said sometimes escaped my mind, which is not so finely edged. His mind was so beautifully and finely edged, and so subtle in its nature, that he went further, and gave us perfect essays in the form of his judgments, which can be handed down to our successors as models of absolute perfection."

It is to be regretted that Bowen should not have enriched the legal literature of his country by any standard work. No one certainly of our day was more qualified to raise any topic out of the dreary level of text-books and reports, to free it from the tangled and bewildering undergrowth of technicalities, and to view law from the dignified standpoint of philosophy.

Bowen's training in the Oxford schools, his speculative turn of mind, his faculty of analysis, his subtlety of thought, all tended to qualify him in the highest degree for handling the subject with the grasp and weight necessary to a philosophic treatise. But his taste strongly disinclined him from any such attempt. He seems to have felt no ambition for, scarcely any belief in, literary success in this direction.

" Is it worth having?" he says in a letter to one of his friends. " I think life is very well worth living. I have no cynical views about it ; but I do not think so very many things are worth having. Especially does the desire to attain immortality by writing a book on English law seem to me a doubtful passion. You write a history of the law, or a treatise about it, and then a puff of reform comes and alters it all, and makes your history or treatise useless. If I were at all able or disposed to write, I am sure that literary art lives longer than mere literary bricks and mortar. Poetry lives as long as most prose ; but, of all prose, a book on English law strikes me as least readable, and most certain to expire by an early death."

However little disposed to engage personally in the scientific treatment of law, Charles Bowen was as far as possible removed from the school of thought which questions the existence of legal science, or, at any rate, its expediency. In January, 1884, he presided at

the annual meeting of the Birmingham Law
Students' Society, and took the opportunity of
enforcing the view—which he himself, an
admiring student of Sir H. Maine, held strongly
—of the value of the historical method as
applied to the Study of the Law.   He drew a
vivid picture of the "dismal, boundless, unknown
land" which presents itself to the pilgrim steps
of the law student.

"Is it possible," he asked, "to introduce a gleam of
sunshine and to furnish a silver thread to guide the
law student through the tangled labyrinth of a law
library?   Wanted, then, a method of studying the
law pleasantly.   Now, I believe that there exists such
a method, absolutely scientific, full of interest, capable
of satisfying the finest intellect, because it affords
a scope for every power.   Law is the application of
certain rules to a subject-matter which is constantly
shifting.   What is it?   English life!   English business!
England in movement, advancing from a continuous
past to a continuous future.   National life, national
business, like every other product of human intelligence and culture, is a growth—begins far away in
the dim past, advances slowly, shaping and forming
itself by the operation of purely natural causes."

N

To this changing subject-matter the rules of law have to be applied—some, mere rules of common sense, fair play, and business convenience; some, specific enactments designed for special cases—but all gradually changing, undergoing an evolution, moving as human intelligence moves, "and taking a colour, form, and elasticity from the nature of transactions to which they are applied."

"The chief difficulty is not so much to discover the principles as to learn how they should be applied. To do this the student has to look for the elements of his art in successive strata, or layers, of authorities, documents, and judicial decisions, each of which is the product of its own particular time, and requires to be studied with reference to it."

From this it follows that the only reasonable, the only satisfactory, way of dealing with law is to bring to bear upon it the historical method.

"Mere legal terminology may seem to you a dead thing. Mix history with it, and it clothes itself with life. You have not even to travel far to find the history to mix. Look for it in the legal material itself; and the history, like water in a fertile soil, is ready there at hand, and will well up into a spring. There before your very eyes, in the fragmentary decisions of the Law Courts, and in the glossaries of Commentators, you will see consecutive chapters of the narrative of the progress of the human race."

To a possible objection that such a view only proved how impossible it is to be a lawyer, Bowen explained that he was not putting forward any Utopian scheme for mastering all law at once, but a mode of arranging such knowledge as we can acquire.

"English law can not be learned in a day. Yet there is all the difference between attacking the study of it on no method at all, and attacking it upon a method which strews flowers over the student's path as he pursues his pilgrimage."

Such a method gives new meaning to all the busy processes of life which the student sees around him, in every direction of human enterprise.

" A study of law so executed will become one full
of interest. Its effect will be to make that study a
living thing, to put life into dead bones, to illuminate
with sunshine dusty books. I am astonished when I
hear at times the suggestion that our profession must
be dull. The truer view would be that our work is
inordinately engrossing. Time runs by the lawyer
far too like the race in a mill-stream. . . . Is the
occupation narrowing to the mind? Can it ever
narrow the mind to learn to perfection the story of
human life? Will it tend to narrow, or to enlarge
the mind to construct for ourselves, in a connected
form, the knowledge of human life, as Englishmen
have pursued it since the memory of English justice?
Science or Art, I care not which it be that challenges
us, I unhesitatingly aver that, followed on the lines
I have endeavoured to sketch out, there is not a
study in the world more exact, more liberal, more
elevating."

Bowen's sense of the dignity and scope of
law made itself apparent in his zealous support
of every scheme for improving the constitution
and procedure of the Courts, by which it is to be
expounded and enforced. No Judge devoted
himself with more assiduity to this branch of
his duties.

In the January number for 1886 of the *Law Quarterly Review*, C. Bowen published an Essay, in which he described the effects of the changes which had been of late effected in the structure and procedure of the Law Courts, and called attention to various points peculiar to the development of the new system which seemed to claim special consideration. The supersession of the historic Courts of the Queen's Bench, Common Pleas, Exchequer, and Exchequer Chamber by a Supreme Court of Judicature, was, no doubt, a wise and necessary reform; but it would, the writer urges, " be a mistake to undervalue the merits of the machinery that we have abandoned, or to suppose that the superior machinery, which has been substituted, is free from its own elements of weakness." The defects of the former system had, no doubt, been remedied by recent reforms, but those very reforms had, in their turn, produced evils which required to be rectified or to be watched. One of the

points incidental to the new *régime,* which
called for consideration, was the serious ac-
cumulation of arrears in the Chancery and
Queen's Bench Divisions. The state of the
cause-list in the Queen's Bench in 1885 made it
obvious that either the number of Judges must
be increased, or that measures should be devised
for a more rapid administration of justice.
The arrears in the Chancery Division were
still more serious. The discussion as to the
most expedient manner of meeting the difficulty
is, necessarily, of a highly technical character,
and scarcely interesting except to those practically conversant with the subject. The article,
however, is interesting as an excellent specimen
of the conscientious thoroughness with which
Bowen thought out every detail of a tiresome
controversy, and of the zeal with which he
elaborated every available means of rendering
the administration of justice as efficient as
possible.

Two other contributions of a like character

may here conveniently be mentioned. In 1887 Mr. Humphrey Ward published, in honour of the Queen's Jubilee, a collection of essays illustrative of the course of development which English Society—science, trade, and the various great Departments of State—had undergone during the preceding fifty years. Lord Justice Bowen contributed a chapter on " The Adminis- tration of the Law," which is an excellent specimen of his style and method in dealing with a professional subject.   He gives a graphic description of the technicalities, confusions, and obscurities which beset litigation at the be- ginning of Queen Victoria's reign, and of the endless delays, ruinous expenditure, and frequent miscarriages of justice to which they conduced.

"From the beginning of the century," he says, "the population, the wealth, the commerce of the country had been advancing by great strides, and the antient bottles were but imperfectly able to hold the new wine. At a moment when the pecuniary enter- prises of the country were covering the world, when railways at home and steam on the seas were creating everywhere new centres of industrial and commercial life, the Common Law Courts of the country seemed constantly occupied in the discussion of the merest legal conundrums, which bore no relation to the merits of any controversies except those of pedants, and in the direction of a machinery that belonged already to the past."

Bowen describes, with all the zest of a law-reformer, the gradual course of improvement till the great measure of 1873 gave the final blow to the old system by the establishment of a Supreme Court, every branch of which administers the same principle of Equity and Law, and is governed by a common and simple procedure. No better summary could be wished ; but the article is more than a summary. It breathes throughout the spirit of a man who shakes himself free from professional prepossessions and prejudice, rises naturally above the level of the subjects amidst which his life is passed, into that higher and more luminous atmosphere where general views present themselves, the gradual processes of growth and development become apparent, and general tendencies and principles can be evolved.

In 1892, again, Bowen rendered an important service to the Profession and the Public by communicating to the Press a dissertation on the scheme of Reform recently forwarded by the Council of Judges to the Home Secretary. The occasion was one of interesting novelty, for it was, probably, "the first time in English history that the entire body of the Judges of the land have approached the Crown with a report on the defects of the present administration of justice, and with a scheme which they have prepared for its improvement."   The right so to report was conferred by the Judicature Act upon the Council.   At the opening of 1892 the Council appointed a Committee ; the Committee sat every day after Court for four months, and its report, with some few alterations, was, after a three days' debate, adopted by the Council.   The proposed reforms

were embodied in a string of resolutions number-
ing about a hundred. They dealt with the whole
subject of Civil Procedure, the arrangements of
the Courts, the Circuit System, the distribution
of Judicial Power, the Question of Appeal, the
undue burthen thrown on the Chancery Judges,
the creation of a special Court for speedy dis-
patch of commercial cases in London, the
procedure in administration suits, declaratory
decrees for the interpretation of deeds or other
documents, the regulation of costs, the review
and control of criminal proceedings and
sentences by appeal or otherwise. The task
of setting forth so wide-reaching, multifarious
and technical a project in language intelligible
to the lay community, and with sufficient lightness and brevity to be endurable by the average
industry of mankind, was no easy one. It fell
to Charles Bowen's lot to perform it, and the
two articles communicated to the *Times*, 1872,
entitled, "The Judges' Reforms, by a Member
of the Bench," give an excellent idea of his

power of exposition, and of the indefatigable diligence with which he had considered every branch of a laborious and, in many respects, unattractive topic.   No man ever worked with more conscientious assiduity at tasks which had nothing in them of a nature to catch the popular eye, or to bring their author into publicity, but which, none the less, tended to render the judicial machinery of the country more conducive to the interests of justice and the convenience of the public.

For many years of his life Charles Bowen was too much absorbed in his professional work to have either leisure, strength, or inclination for Society.   His days, and too often his nights, were occupied in the painful endeavour to keep pace with ever-increasing demands for his services either in Court, or as an adviser on questions of legal difficulty.   After his elevation to the Bench, his failing health offered frequent impediments to social intercourse, except within a restricted circle.   For some years, however, after his elevation to the Bench, Bowen found opportunities of enjoying the pleasures of sociability.   In 1878 he had been elected a member of the Athenæum, and in 1880 of the Literary Society, and of Grillon's.   He was also a member of the "Dilettanti," and of "The Club."   Sir M. E. Grant Duff gives us glimpses of many pleasant scenes which Bowen's presence helped to make pleasanter— dinners at Grillon's and the Literary Society, visits to Hampden, Sundays at York House, afternoon gossips at the Athenæum—faint and ghostly echoes of a world from which so many who did most to enliven it have already passed away !   Bowen's brilliant talk, ready sympathy, playfulness, wit, and personal charm made him a welcome guest in circles where his graver intellectual powers would hardly have been understood or appreciated.   He could always be amusing, and humanity is thankful to any one who can and will amuse it.   There is a natural and laudable craving for something

better, brighter, more interesting than the
ordinary level of social intercourse. Of Charles
Bowen's charm no one who came within the
sphere of his attractions could have a doubt.
His witty sayings passed from mouth to mouth.
He became in great request. His presence
was supposed to ensure the brilliancy of an
entertainment. Accomplished hostesses, whose
business it is to organize brilliant entertain-
ments, marked him for their own. Bowen was
not insensible to such an appeal. His strain
of Irish blood disposed him to sociability. He
felt the interest and excitement of conversation.
He formed many agreeable acquaintances,
several much-valued friendships. Congenial
companionship is the best of all anodines for
harassing anxieties, the tedium of professional
work, and the depressing consciousness of an
impaired constitution and failing health. Bowen
enjoyed the society of his species with the zest
of a sensitive and sympathetic nature, unspoiled
by self-indulgence, and safe-guarded through its

perilous epoch by pure taste and an austere
standard ; but Society was with him but an
episode, not perhaps an important episode, in
a busy career ; it formed no part of his more
serious existence.   From the outer world that
serious side was carefully concealed.   Those
who knew him but superficially found it
difficult to believe that so much brilliancy and
such ever-ready fun could be combined with
gravity of thought, a profound philosophy of
life, and a deep undercurrent of melancholy.
But playfulness is oftentimes a natural precaution
against being tempted to reveal the bitterness
which each man's heart knows, and in which
he wishes no companionship.   Charles Bowen
was, it may be, sometimes the victim of such a
mood.   He shrank, even with his intimate
friends, from handling serious topics, and
sometimes, when conversation threatened to
invade the domain in which he preferred to
maintain an unbroken reticence, would divert
it into a less serious channel by a remark

that seemed to disappointed listeners merely
frivolous. It was not frivolity, however, which
was the motive cause of his behaviour, but a
sense of the importance of such topics, the
magnitude and solemnity of the issues involved,
the superficial and inadequate treatment which
they must receive in any general gathering,
however carefully selected.

Some of the occasions on which Bowen's
gifts of sociability showed themselves to the
greatest advantage were the dinners of the
" Literary Society," at whose monthly dinners,
presided over by Lord Coleridge, many of
Bowen's intimate associates were accustomed
to assemble. Among its frequenters were Mr.
George S. Venables, himself a distinguished
proficient in the art of good conversation, Hon.
George Denman, a scholar of high traditional
fame, Mr. Spencer Walpole, who is now, as
was his father before him, president of the
Club, Sir James Fitzjames Stephen, Mr. Lecky,
Mr. Birrell, Sir M. E. Grant Duff, Canon

Liddon, Canon Ainger, the Dean of Westminster, Sir A. Lyall, Mr. Henry James, Mr.
G. Du Maurier, and Mr. Sidney Colvin, whose
rights as *arbiter bibendi* entitled him to rule
the feast with despotic authority.   Lord Coleridge, certainly one of the best *raconteurs* of
his day, did full justice to the presidential
chair.   Stimulated by congenial surroundings,
he would pour out his reminiscences of Bar
and Bench and Parliament in an unfailing and,
apparently, inexhaustible stream of graphic
narrative.   When he and Bowen sat on
opposite sides of the table, and got to capping
each other's stories, the listeners were sure of
an interesting half-hour.   Both had had some
curious experiences of Lord Westbury, which
lost nothing in the telling.   I remember sometimes thinking that no single personage of his
generation can have afforded more amusement
to his species than that versatile and accomplished lawyer.   But how to recall such scenes
or depict them ?   Yesterday's unfinished bottle

of champagne is but a feeble representation of
the staleness of the written record of transient
hilarity. The essence of fun is to be spontaneous, apposite, and instantaneous. Caught
between the solemn pages of a book, and stuck,
like a butterfly with a pin through its back in
a well-camphored tray for the purposes of
science or curiosity, it is but the dead sem-
blance of itself. Many of the good things
which sent Bowen's companions away with the
impression of having been infinitely amused,
require the setting of the bland, mock-modest
manner, and hesitating utterance with which
they were produced, and the smile of genuine
enjoyment by which they were accompanied.
Some of the Literary Society diners will
remember the gravity with which, some one
having mentioned a work, entitled " Defence
of the Church of England, By a beneficed
clergyman," Bowen suggested, " In other words,
a defence of the Thirty-nine Articles by a *bonâ
fide* holder for value." On another occasion

o

reference was made to the fact that a publisher, who was popularly credited with driving somewhat hard bargains with authors, had built a church at his own expense. "Ah!" Bowen exclaimed, "the old story! *Sanguis martyrum semen Ecclesiæ.*" Sometimes his wit could turn a dexterous compliment, as when he assured some ladies, who had been climbing to perilous eminence on an Alpine crag, that they had solved the problem, which had perplexed the Schoolmen, as to how many angels could stand on the point of a needle. Sometimes a satiric touch. Some of the pleasure-hunting invalids at Homburg remember an observation of Lord Bowen's that a little dog, whose attendance on its Royal Master was not as faithful as might have been wished, was the only person at Homburg who did not run after the Prince of Wales.

Bowen's vivacity, gaiety, and ready wit—his gentle irony never hardening into sarcasm —his flashes of humour, were naturally much appreciated in professional circles, and in that judicial Olympus, whose sublimity, it is not profane to imagine, may sometimes stand in need of a little enlivenment. Many such good stories live in the traditions of the Bar. Bowen's contemporaries recall an occasion on which the draft of an address to Royalty was being considered by the Judges. It contained the expression, "Conscious as we are of our shortcomings." Exception was taken to the phrase as pitched in too humble a key. No such consciousness, it was urged, besets the judicial mind. "Suppose," Bowen demurely suggested, "that we substitute 'Conscious as we are of one another's short-comings'?"

Equally amusing was Bowen's reply to one of the Judges, who was complaining that another member of the Bench had slept peacefully through the afternoon, and, on waking up at half-past three, had immediately adjourned the Court. "It is as it should be," Bowen said.

He obeyed the hymn, "Shake off dull sloth, and early rise." Of one of his colleagues, whose temperament showed some want of masculine robustness, Bowen observed, "I do not know whether to speak of him as my learned brother or my learned sister." On another occasion, one of the Judges having complained that he did not know what a "Jurist" meant, Bowen proceeded to give a definition. "A Jurist," he said, "is a person who knows a little about the laws of every country except his own."

A flash of gentle fun shows itself occasionally in Bowen's judgments. "Had I been left to myself," he said, in dealing with a case in which the Court below had shown a perverse ingenuity in misconstruing a document, "I should have thought—the judgment of the learned Judge shows me that I should have been wrong—that it was impossible to mis-understand this letter." "Her Majesty's Courts," he observed in a case, in which an attempt was made to defeat the plaintiff's claim on the ground of an irregularity in procedure, "do not exist for the purposes of discipline, but for the decision of disputes between the subjects."

Recorded *bons mots*, however, are but the mummies of wit—records of the living man, but with a sepulchral aroma. As he said of Professor Henry Smith, "the brightest conversation is often the most evanescent, and the *finesse* of wit, like a musical laugh, disappears with the occasion, and cannot be reproduced on paper or in print." The Bowen whom I remember, and would fain delineate, sparkling with genial and charming gaiety, lives better in familiar letters, never intended for any but the recipient's eye, or for any but an ephemeral existence. Mr. Justice Mathew kindly allows me to quote one or two, in which Bowen's natural gaiety seems to play at ease.

" My dear J. C.,

"I am convalescent, and shall be again at the Owlary next term; but, as usual, in low spirits. Beef-tea—such is my experience (I believe the liquid was invented by your illustrious uncle) is a chastening beverage. I return a sobered man; and if I am at Greenwich on the 20th I shall bring my own teapot, and sit on the balcony (during dinner) by myself. As for Politics — the Parnell Commission — the Common Law—Equity—Literature—Art—Science —they are all very unimportant subjects of thought and reflection to one who has had to live on beef-tea and to think of his immortal soul. I will not, therefore, offer any observations to you upon these or any other worldly topics.

"Remember me to Dasent, and to Lyall at the Athenæum; and, as you will probably receive this when you are on your way to the Courts, let me say once for all that I am an Equity Lawyer, and that jokes at the expense of Chitty, Cozens Hardy, or Mr. Justice Kekewich, are all equally misplaced. Give my love and esteem to Chitty. I do not call him a *sound* Equity Lawyer, but a painstaking one. I will play him a single-wicket match on Blackheath Common before dinner on the 20th for a sovereign, and let him have Manisty to field.

" It has turned very cold here. But it *was* delicious,

all sorts of flowers blooming and smelling as sweet as 'anythink.'

"Good-bye. Bless you. Remember me to the Chief. 'Be good, my lords, and let who will be clever.' Take this for your and Grantham's motto when you sit together, deciding questions of Habeas Corpus.

"Yours always,

"C. B.

"Billæus Rogerius writes that he has become a Sheriff's Chaplain, and, as such, has got a box of first-rate cigars. I shall be *There* betimes. Snuff and smoke. *Voila la vie! Pulvis et Umbra sumus!*"

The following request for a lift in his friend's carriage to the Lord Chancellor's breakfast in 1883 sinks below the dignity of history. I shall, I think, be forgiven for the lapse.

"Colwood, Hayward Heath, Sussex.

"My dear J. C.,
   Will you be free
   To carry me
   Beside of thee,
   In your Buggee,
   To Selborne's Tea?
   If breakfast He

Intends for we
On 2 November next, D.V.
Eighteen hundred Eighty Three
A. D.
For Lady B.
From Cornwall G.
Will absent Be,
And says that She
Would rather see
Her husband be—
D dash dash D—
Than send to London Her Buggee
For such a melancholy spree
As Selborne's Toast and Selborne's Tea."

"What a libel on me," is added in a feminine hand, and signed " F. B."

The " Athenæum " Club is popularly regarded as a serious institution, but here are a couple of letters, arranging symposia within its walls, which have an agreeable ring of fun.

" Saturday night.

"MY DEAR J. C.,
          " Pax tecum, Archimagister bibendi !   Don't forget you are WELBY'S and MY GUEST Tuesday 8 p.m., Athenæum, to meet the G.O.M.

"Other guests—Archbishop of Canterbury, American Minister, F. Leveson-Gower, Millais, Burnand, Du Maurier, Strong (a great Orientalist scholar; please talk to him, for he will know nobody), Alfred Morrison (probably), Robert Herbert (possibly).

"I shall *not* be there. My doctor won't hear of it. He has sent me to Colwood to-morrow (Sunday) by midday train.

"You quite comprehend, it is not an 'Ouse' dinner, but Welby's and *my* dinner."

"My dear J. C.,

"Hope you are not in prison, but it looks like it. I see Dillon is.

"Is your throat better? I got a 'casual' to take your place at the dinner, but who could adequately fill it ! ! ! So you will have nothing to pay, which may console you. We missed you much.

"C. Bowen."

Here is a specimen of the sort of Latin in which famous scholars correspond.

"Beate Sancte 'Matthia,'

"Tu es, quod dicunt, 'Trumpa,' et ego gratias tibi ago. Cigarri sunt excellentissimi. At non ego volo (nam ambo pauperes diaboli sumus) accipere tuâ expensâ boxum tuum. Ergo si

tobacconistæ tui mihi mittent duos alteros boxos, ego
remittem iis checkum pro tribus boxis; et animum
meum liberavero ergo te.

"Accipe gratias meas mille tempora ; et, quanquam
Inquisitionem redoles, et Guyam Fawxum moribus
refers, nihilominus te multum diligo ; et tuus amicus
(salvâ salute animi) semper remanebo.

"C. B."

On another occasion a festive evening is
proposed. "Postquam dimidium maris transi-
tum," adds the writer, as he goes on to describe
what is to be the programme at this hilarious
stage of the proceedings.

Charles Bowen's translation of the "Eclogues"
of Virgil and the first six books of the "Æneid,"
published in 1887, took all but a very small
circle of intimate friends by surprise. It had
been the amusement of his leisure hours during
the Long Vacations and other intervals of
leisure for several years past—the amusement,
the solace, sometimes, it must be feared, too
much of a burthen. It is certain that this, as
every other piece of work which Lord Bowen

undertook, was performed with all the conscientious and exquisite diligence which was
his natural mood.   No one, he confided to an
intimate friend, would ever have an idea of the
amount of toil which it had involved.   Hours
had often been spent over a single line which
proved refractory against the process of translation.

Many of Virgil's most beautiful lines are
untranslatable.   Some are more beautiful in
sound than in idea, and can not be made
melodious in English without betraying their
poverty of meaning.   Others, lovely alike in
sense and sound, are too delicate to bear trans-
planting.   Bowen himself was aware of the
perilous difficulty of the task.   "A translator
of Virgil into English verse," he says, "finds
the road, along which he has undertaken to
travel, strewn with the bleaching bones of
unfortunate pilgrims who have preceded him."
He lays down, as axiomatic, that a translation
of the "Æneid," to be of any value, must be in

itself an English poem, and the English poem, in its turn, must be a translation, not merely a paraphrase.   Tried by these tests "most Virgilian versifiers have perished in the wilderness."   Dryden's rendering—noblest and most masculine of all—scarcely gives us more than a paraphrase.   " He has taken Virgil into his powerful grasp, crushed him to atoms, and reproduced the fragments in a form which, though not devoid of genius, is no longer Virgil's. The silver trumpet has disappeared, and a manly strain is breathed through bronze."   Professor Conington's translation—scholar-like, accurate, and skilful—shocks the reader by the substitution of a metre and manner as remote as possible from that of Virgil.   " The sweet and solemn majesty of the ancient form is wholly gone.   All that is left is what Virgil might have written if the 'Æneid' had been a poem of the character of ' Marmion ' or ' The Lay of the Last Minstrel.' "

But the translation, as Bowen conceived

it, involved a further requirement. Educated
Englishmen have been fed upon Virgil from
boyhood upwards : " Hundreds of Virgil's lines
are familiar quotations, which linger in our
memory, and round which our literary associations cluster and hang, as religious sentiment
clings to well-known texts in the Bible." The
charm of association is lost, unless there be a
" corresponding English line, pointed and complete in itself, containing, however imperfectly,
the plan of the original." The translation
should, therefore, be *lineal* as well as literal. In
what English metre can these requirements be
best satisfied ? The standard English metres
are too short for the purpose. The English
hexameter, with its final dissyllabic foot
shortened to a monosyllable, seemed to Bowen
the best solution. This admitted of rhyme,
in which habit has accustomed the English
ear to take pleasure. Of the merits of this
metre, as "susceptible of varied treatment,
full of flexibility, capable of rising to real

grandeur," Bowen was thoroughly convinced,
though he dared not claim for it that it preserved the orderly and majestic movement
of the Roman hexameter, or allowed of a consistent imitation of the Latin cadence. · It
was the best, however, of which the English
language allowed. On this, and on the merits
of the translation, it is for scholars to pronounce. Of all forms of foolish criticism, none
seems more futile and impertinent than the
offhand judgment, summarily pronounced on
literary workmanship of an elaborate and
exquisite order—the result of long-sustained
intellectual effort. No one certainly is competent to express an opinion on such a translation as this, who has not drunk deep of the
Pierian spring, and studied the original poem
in the reverential and appreciative spirit in
which Bowen addressed himself to the task.
Every line, it may be assumed, is as good
as skill, scholarship, the finest literary taste,
and a fervent spirit of literary endeavour could

make it. No toil was spared, and no amount of time. But, then, toil and time struggle in vain with impossibility, and some lines of Virgil are to a translator, with Lord Bowen's aim and standard, impossible. The poem fascinated him as it has fascinated so many highly gifted natures at every stage of European culture. It was fitting that

"Old Virgil, who would write ten lines, they say,
At dawn, and lavish all the golden day
To make them wealthier in his readers' eyes,"

should be rendered to a modern audience by an interpreter who, with every other qualification for the task, was ready to devote long days, and burn the midnight oil, in giving every detail of his work the necessary polish. A highly gratified critic, Professor W. G. Sellar, of Edinburgh,* expressed, in no hesitating terms, his view of the degree in which Bowen had achieved success.

* *Classical Review*, March, 1888.

"He combines in a higher degree than any of those who have previously attempted the task, the two requisites of finished scholarship, and of power, versatility, and delicacy in the use of language and metre. No one, however familiar with the language of Virgil, can compare passages in this English version, line by line, and phrase by phrase, with the original, without apprehending much that was in the poet's mind, which he had not perceived before, and without feeling his power and charm with a new enjoyment. The exact and refined scholarship of the translator shows itself in the minute carefulness of his workmanship, and his fidelity to the subtle suggestions and shades of meaning in the original. But to accurate scholarship and critical appreciation he adds the lively susceptibility, the mobility of mind and imagination, the affluence of language, and the power, care, and tact in its employment, characteristic of a literary artist; and, with these gifts of an artistic temperament, he combines acuteness and soundness of judgment derived from the education of a great practical career."

Professor Sellar, though not so ardent an admirer as Bowen of a shortened rhyming hexameter, yet considers that "it reproduces, as well as any metre could, the simpler, more lively, and buoyant movement of the "Eclogues."

It can do justice not only to their softer cadences, but to the deeper tones which his sympathy with the grander voices of Nature elicits from the poet—

"Neither the whispering breeze of the south wind, now on its
    way,
Brings me a joy thus deep, nor the thunders of surf on the
    shore,
Nor when the rock-strewn valley resounds to the torrent's
    roar."

In regard to the "Æneid," both metre and manner are, Professor Sellar considered, "more fitted to do justice to it as a poem of heroic adventure, of human sensibility and passion, of descriptive power, of great finish and detail, than as the expression of the Imperial sentiment and character of Rome—'the stateliness and majesty,' as he elsewhere expresses it, 'of some of the more "Imperial" passages. . . .'" Let experts decide. Be the shortcomings of the metre what they may, it will not, I think, be denied that, in Lord Bowen's hands, it was susceptible, on occasion, of a solemn grandeur and pathos which well became the scene, on which were displayed the destinies of an Imperial race.

Bowen himself was fully conscious of the key in which the patriotic passages of the poem must be pitched. They spoke to a Roman audience with the meaning and significance of a very personal interest. " To appreciate the Æneid truly, it is necessary to think of it always as written for the ears of a people who had risen to be masters of the world, after an internecine struggle, out of which Carthage, long mistress of the seas, and redoubtable to Rome even upon land, had at one time nearly emerged triumphant, and in which Rome had nearly perished." Dis aliter visum. The hand of Heaven pointed unwaveringly, through a long series of vicissitudes, to the predestined climax—the majestic and benign presidency of Rome over a conquered and submissive world. In the sixth book of the "Æneid" this splendid climax is kept constantly in sight. It is, says the translator, the noblest passage in Latin literature. Æneas, carrying in his person the fortunes of his race, visits the ghostly world, passes to the Elysian fields, discovers his father among the ranks of the blest, and learns from him the mystery of that second life, to which the purified soul, after ages of purgation, will return to live on earth. In a majestic procession the projected shadows of kings and warriors pass—Cæsar, Pompey, Augustus: the gorgeousness of the scene melts in the pathos of the boy Marcellus—a nation's hope and love —destined to die on the verge of manhood. Amid the splendour of a court ceremonial there breaks in the touch of Nature, and the mother, Octavia, is carried away, fainting, from the scene. The episode is among the most striking, interesting, and pathetic of any which classical history presents. Nor is the translation unworthy of the noble language in which the original rises to a sublime occasion.

The first hours of the translation's existence were not without their vicissitudes.

" Fancy what might have happened!" Charles Bowen
writes to his wife, May, 24, 1884; " I was working in
the library at the Athenæum, into a volume of my
Virgil, the 'Eclogues.' Going home, I forgot all about
it ; it was 11 p.m.; nor did I think of my volume for
three days after, when suddenly I recollected that I
had not brought it home.   What *had* I done with it ?
In a most melancholy frame of mind, I walked over
to the Athenæum. There in the hall an advertisement—

> ' Found in the Library a MS. Quarto Book
> containing poetry.'

What do you think of that for an extra humiliation
thrown in quite casually by Providence ? I had to
go and claim my beloved waif-and-stray with my tail
between my legs ; and now I feel that even the hall-
porter says to himself : ' That a Lord Justice ! why,
he writes poetry ! ' Good-bye, my dearest."

For any sustained effort in original poetry
Charles Bowen's busy life afforded no opportunity. But his keen poetical sense and perfect
mastery of language naturally prompted him,
as occasion offered and the inspiring mood came
on, to poetical composition. A small collection
of these scattered pieces was formed some

years before his death, but he never allowed them to pass into the hands of any but a few intimate friends. To such they are of great interest; not, of course, as in any way adequate representations of his literary power, but as recalling the grace and sweetness—the fastidious taste, the fine ear for musical cadence, the gay and melancholy moods, the playfulness with its undercurrent of deep feeling, which they remember as characteristic of him and his work. They bear the impress of their origin,—fugitive, desultory, fragmentary, and, it may be, of unequal merit; but to the understanding ear—especially to the ear of friendship—they have a music and a pathos of their own. They are in no sense autobiographic; but none the less indicate various phases of sentiment, to which Charles· Bowen felt moved from time to time to give poetic form.

In one he strikes the note of the ambitious and aspiring mind, checked and abashed by the fast-approaching end.

" Life and new life—Give me the cup once more.
No need to crown for me its rim with flowers—
These would but bring again the scent of hours
Too sweet to scorn, too fleeting to deplore.
Youth's triumphs—revel—joys in golden store—
Rich love itself hath brought me poor content,
For the grey thought that, ere the wine be spent,
Night comes apace to close the festal door.
Let boys wreath fate with lilies ; I, aflame
To do what yet I know not, strive a strife,
Smite once in thunder at all doors of fame,
And make dull worlds re-echo ; ask but life,
To slake this thirst, and be what men have been,
Ere I go hence, and am no longer seen."

In another he drops the plummet into the
void, and shows human love in a gloomy but
not unheroic phase.

"TO HERMIONE.

" Hermione, you ask me if I love ;
And I do love you.   But indeed we drift
Fast by the flying, fleeting banks of life
Towards the inevitable seas.   It seems
But yesterday I saw, as in a dream,
Childhood—a flame of glory—come and go.
And, lo ! to-day these hairs are flecked with time
Already ; and all the silver minutes glide
More dreamily than ever for the love
I bear you : hand in hand, and hour by hour,

Floating beside you to the sounding falls,
Whence we must leap together into night.
Are we not happy? Is not life serene?
We do but pass, you say, from one bright shore
Upon a brighter! Dear Hermione,
Be glad there is no shadow on your eyes ;
But this I know, that all the world beside
Seems faint with pain ; the rose upon your breast
Is not more full of perfume than the world
Of pain. I hear it even at your side
By day and night—the illimitable sigh
Breathed upward to the throne of the deaf skies—
A cry of hollow-cheeked and hungry men
Burning away life's fire for little ends ;
And women with wan hearts and starving eyes
Waiting for those they love to come again
From strange embraces—ruined womanhood
And barren manhood, fruitful but of pain.
Such is the shore we float from ; for the shore,
The brighter shore, we reach, I only know
That it is night, Hermione, mere night,
Unbroken, unillumined, unexplored.
Come closer, lay your hand in mine ; your love
Is the one sure possession that will last.
Let us be brave, and when the Shadow comes
To beckon us to the leap, rise lightly up
And follow with firm eyes and resolute soul
Whither he leads—one heart, one hand, to live
Together, or, if Death be Death, to die."

In another, conceived in a very different
mood, but with equal charm and grace, we find

friendship reassuring its recipient, and protest-
ing with elaborate, perhaps not unnecessary,
emphasis, that it is not love.

> " Go, Song, and fall at Silvia's feet, and say
>   Thou art not Love—but from a frozen sky
>   That knows not of Love's name nor of Love's way,
>   Hast fluttered idly to her door to die.
>   Shake from thy plumes, before thou meet her eye,
>   All passion—veil thy gaze, forget thy pain,
>   And, if she take thee on her heart to lie,
>   Become a thing of beauty—a soft strain
>   Filling her dreams with music.   Should she deign
>   To ask what bird, in what enchanted grove,
>   Taught thee a note so tender, swear again,
>   By all thou holdest dear, it was not Love ;
>   Else she will drive thee, Song, into the night,
>   And lost my toil will be and thy delight."

Some of the love-songs have a Tennysonian
ring, but are none the less charming for their
frankly imitative form.   For instance

" GOOD NIGHT, GOOD MORNING.

> " The Sun, a shining orb, descends
>   Behind the mountain wold ;
>   Gloom gathers fast, the daylight ends ;
>   Sheep journey to the fold.

Peace and farewell, ye torrent rills—
  Good night to earth and sky.
So homeward from the silent hills
  We went, my love and I.
Come, sweet night.   Day, take thy flight :
My love will make the darkness light.

" Rest to the earth—the weary earth—
  Sweet rest : till far away
Upon the hills we saw the birth
  And triumph of the day.
Again the mighty sun arose,
  And on each mountain lawn
Began the million golden glows
  That usher in the dawn.
Go, dear night.   Come, purple light ;
Rise, Love, and make the morning bright.

"At noon I found these violets blue
  Where early morning lies,
And brought them fresh with light and dew—
  Not purer than her eyes—
To her who was my morning flower,
  As is my flower of noon.
Soon comes a duskier twilight hour,
  And night will follow soon.
Sweet face, stay : life ebbs away,
Be thou thy lover's evening ray."

On rare occasions Bowen addressed a general
audience on topics which lay outside the domain
of law.   One of them was in December, 1888,

when he distributed the prizes at the City
of London School, and took the opportunity
of remarking on a controversy which was
attracting attention—the value of examinations
as an educational method, and of the crammer,
the object at the moment of somewhat un-
reasonable objurgation.   He told a good story
of a complaint of Chief Justice Cockburn that
an aged charwoman, whose duty it was to light
the fires in the Judge's rooms, had been carried
off by the Treasury in her declining years to
undergo a Civil Service examination.   There
is a natural feeling that "an Englishman's
ignorance, like his house, is his castle—a kind
of South Africa which ought to be closed to
explorers."   As matters stand, the crammer—
though he does not come across the path
of the real student, the real artist, or the real
man of science—is not without his uses.
"Cramming is the tribute which idleness pays
to the excellence of industry.   The crammer
does his best for his pupil.   He may over-

load him, but he produces him, after all, in the condition desired by the market."

In 1891, again, Bowen addressed the Walsall Literary Society, and selected novel-reading as his topic. Some touches recall the sort of talk with which Bowen would amuse a congenial circle.

"Few writers," he says, "have painted the outside and, so far as there is an inside, the inside of ordinary insipid characters better than Mr. Trollope. . . ."

"Eugène Sue was not fit either to serve in heaven or reign in hell. His distinct mediocrity of taste was redeemed by wit, and enlivened by a kindly epicurean familiarity with the world. The least superficial quality he possessed was his frivolity, which sinks to a considerable depth, though his other powers are more easily exhausted."

George Sand's self-consciousness is glanced at as a shortcoming of genius.

"The authoress who wishes to outlive her contemporaries must first learn to outlive her own *malaise.*" "Love-making," he observes elsewhere, "seems to have been a natural taste even in the primitive days ; but our modern familiarity with its phenomena is partly due to the continuous exertions of novelists. Much of love has only been learnt under the instruction of some woman who has herself only learnt it from a book."

He combats the realistic theory that " the literary workman is entitled to portray the pigsties of Epicurus, provided that the colouring is masterly, the composition skilful, and the pigs true to nature."

"The end of scientific inquiry is, unquestionably, truth ; but the literature of the imagination is an art, not a science, and its object is not truth, but the truthful presentation of beauty, and of other conceptions, which are really suited for the pen. Authors are not bound by any divine law of their being to surprise truth in all her hiding-places. Nor is it necessary that everything should be described in romance, any more than in real life it is the duty of everybody to be photographed. . . . It is not the absence of costume, but the presence of innocence which makes the Garden of Eden."

On another occasion, in 1893, Charles Bowen addressed a gathering of students of the Working Men's College, Great Ormond Street, an institution in which he had, thirty-two years before, taken an active interest. He now broke a friendly lance with Professor Mahaffy, who had been saying some gloomy and disrespectful things about popular education. The address sparkles with flashes of the fun which played, like an electric flame, over Charles Bowen's most serious mood. He gives the Dublin Professor a little gentle satire on his undue pessimism; but he evidently is to a large degree in sympathy with his views.

"The first result of a great educational movement is a general diffusion of mediocre knowledge, and it is idle to expect a literary millennium at once to set in. Till recently intelligence ran in a restricted channel between boundaries that were ungenerously narrow. The river has broken its banks and overwhelmed the land; it sweeps in a sounding sea over the plains, and one can not be surprised that it does not flow everywhere at its old depth. At such periods in the onward march, a great deal is said, done, and written that is below the level of creditable learning. The noise of newly emancipated tongues drowns the still small voice of culture. High standards are not recognized, or cease to be impressive; the quality of the supply is affected by the quantity of the demand, since cheap thought, like light claret, can be produced on an extensive scale. The highways and byways of literature are given up, so to speak, to the literary bicyclist. He travels in a costume peculiar to himself, and he considers the landscape as his own. Expressions of violence are employed to describe commonplace emotions. Towards individuals we practise the same indistinctness of judgment, the same indifference to proportion. We pursue successful men and women to their down-setting and uprising; we enjoy descriptions of their household furniture. Memorials are erected to every one who will only die in the odour of respectability. We write long biographies of nobody, and we celebrate the centenaries of nothing."

Culture is naturally alarmed at the inroad of Gothic hordes into regions sacred to literature and art, and at the turmoil incidental to the invasion.

"One can even conceive of the most brilliant professors at our Universities, under the influence of temporary disquietude, jealously and suspiciously mounting guard over their own educational blessings, as if they were keeping an eye on their luggage at a crowded railway station."

It is unfair, however, to criticize the inevitable incompleteness of a new system with microscopic exactness.

"The bystander will misjudge the significance of the change, if he concentrates his attention on the roughness and unsightliness of the rude building-plots on which the edifices of the future have only begun to be laid out. Reforms have, as a rule, to be purchased at some sacrifice of the luxurious quiet and picturesque amenity to which the past has been accustomed, just as a railway interferes with the seclusion of the village or the beauty of the valley."

But the education from which real ennoblement may be hoped must not be estimated from the commercial and mechanical point of view.

"Instruction ladled out in a hurry is not education. The cultivation for market purposes of brute brain power has its uses, public and private; but the market advantages of education are not the criterion of its value to individuals or the nation. To teach the young generation to snatch greedily at mental improvement, with the sole purpose of disposing at a profit of what they learn, is to narrow and injure education. Education must not be regarded as a mere ladder of advancement and advertisement, as a

means of pushing, in front of others, into an inner
circle, where the good things of this life are being
given away. Egotism will spoil education as it spoils
religion and as it spoils ethics. All three lose their
virtue and medicinal efficacy when selfishness settles
down upon them like a fog. Education does not
mean the knowing a little more Latin or Greek than
one's neighbour, or the application, for pecuniary
purposes, of a superior polish to one's own brains.
Its true purport and mission were discovered by
those who conferred on learning the name of 'the
humanities,' based on the conception of universal
sympathy with mankind. Education, touched by
this principle, ceases to be a personal struggle, and
becomes an illumination—a training based on the
sense of human fraternity. Thus conceived, it is
desired as the best means of sharing the great
thoughts of the past, and comprehending the hopes
of the future. The point at which it kindles and
ennobles is where we first reach the atmosphere of
great men, great deeds, great ideas. Up to this
moment knowledge may have been a delicate luxury,
the satisfaction of a taste, the indulgence of a curious
passion. From and after such a moment we live,
not in ourselves, but in the fellowship of the greatest
thinkers and the best men. The story of the world,
thereupon, lights up into a narrative of evolution—a
story of the conflicts and triumphs of freedom,
heroism, and truth. And, whatever be the ultimate

catastrophes of the universe, they will not have obscured for us the spectacle, on this tiny and perishable planet, of an unwearying race, of which we ourselves are part, still linked together in prospective and retrospective sympathy, still pressing onward, still nursing the sacred fire, still cherishing ideals, still hoping for perfection."

From his appointment as a Lord Justice of Appeal to his promotion to the House of Lords, in 1893, Bowen's life was of the same laborious and uneventful tenor as in its earlier stages. The claims of the Court of Appeal were imperative and continuous. The judgments there delivered—authoritative declarations of English law—sometimes clearing away obscurities, sometimes correcting mistakes of long standing, sometimes modifying an old rule in its application to new and altered conditions, necessitated the utmost care, erudition, and research, and left but scanty leisure for other interests. Occasionally, the chance of a holiday presented itself. In 1883 the Canadian Pacific Railway Company invited a party of

Q

distinguished Englishmen to travel over its line, and enjoy its splendid hospitality. Lord Coleridge, Hannen, and Charles Bowen were of the party. The expedition was not, so far as Bowen was concerned, altogether a success. Everything that hospitality could suggest for the comfort of the guests was, of course, forthcoming. Unluckily, it was impossible to preclude accidents, and two accidents occurred. On both occasions Bowen underwent a shaking, for which his nerves were very ill prepared; on the second, the train broke away from the engine and ran down an incline, and the travellers had to save themselves from an impending smash by jumping off the train, as occasion offered. Not feeling well enough for a journey diversified by such vicissitudes, Bowen broke off from the party, and travelled slowly home by himself, not much the better, thanks to these mishaps, for his two crossings of the Atlantic.

In February, 1885. Bowen received tidings

of a compliment which, I believe, gave him greater pleasure than any of the honours which had fallen to his lot.   The master of Balliol wrote :—

"MY DEAR LORD JUSTICE,

"I have the pleasure of announcing to you that the College, in the exercise of this singular privilege, yesterday elected you Visitor, if you are willing to undertake the duties of that, not very troublesome, office.

"We are all very glad of the election (which was unanimous) and no one more than I am.

"Ever yours affectionately,

"B. JOWETT."

Early in 1890 Charles Bowen sustained a great sorrow in the death of Alexander Craig Sellar, one of his oldest and most valued friends. Few losses could have cost him more.   Sellar's cheery and genial temperament, which enabled him to render such important services to his party in the House of Commons, made him in private life the best of companions.   No man could tell a story better, or had a more

unfailing supply on hand; his Parliamentary
experience had brought him into contact with
many men, and his native shrewdness and
insight had turned his opportunities to the
best account.   But, with him, mirth was ever
mellowed with kindliness, and those who knew
him most intimately had the strongest sense
of his goodness of heart, his chivalrous sense
of honour, and the sincere kindness of nature
which gave a charm to his society.   His health
had for long been uncertain and failing, and
the strain of his Parliamentary life hastened
the collapse.   In the summer of 1889, he went
to Homburg, but only to return a dying man.
Several months of suffering ensued, and in the
spring of 1890 the end came.   Throughout the
illness Charles Bowen's continuous letters of
gossip and affection had done much to cheer
his friend.   He was at this time himself in
extremely bad health.   He had been attacked
by the prevailing epidemic of influenza, and
suffered a long and painful illness.   The disease

affected the nerves of the eye, and gave him many weeks of acute suffering. He was greatly prostrated, and his general health received a serious shock. When, at last, he was sufficiently recovered to allow of his removal to Colwood, the change seemed to work but little good. At times he would brighten up, and talk with something of his accustomed gaiety and zest; but he underwent frequent relapses. It was at last resolved to try the experiment of a sojourn on the Riviera. His old friend, Mr. Bullock Hall, was residing at Valescure, and offered him and Lady Bowen a cordial welcome. Subsequently, the Bowens moved into another villa, which the kindness of a friend placed at their disposal, where, a little later, he heard of his father's death, at Bordighera, the consequence of an attack of influenza. Mr. Bowen was now in his eighty-ninth year, and had, up to the last, preserved his powers, mental and physical, unimpaired.

In March, 1890, Professor Jowett writes

to Charles Bowen with reference to these events.

" MY DEAR BOWEN,

        " I was going to write to you, as I have
been any time during the last six weeks, when I saw
in the paper the death of your venerable father. I
fear that you have had a great deal of trouble lately ;
but I hardly count this as a trouble, for he was a most
excellent man, and lived beyond the usual term,
and he was very happy, and a great part of his happiness was your distinction and success. And now he
is—where we all shall be some day—with God.

    " Since we met, we have also lost another dear
friend, about whom I shall have much to say to you
when we see one another again. Your words were
the greatest comfort to him and to his family.

    " What I am chiefly anxious about is your health.
You have had a very long and depressing illness, and
must have had the thoughts which usually accompany
such an illness. I suppose that resignation is an
alternative which has sometimes crossed your mind.
I hope that you will exhaust all the possibilities of
rest and vacation before you have recourse to this
dernier ressort. But, if you should be unable to go
on at present, do not look at the prospect as at all
desperate. You will have leisure for reading and
thinking, and probably the opportunity of using your

great legal faculty in the House of Lords—more liberty, and, therefore, more force for any purpose.

" I fear that I must have seemed very negligent of you in your trouble, when I think of all the regard and affection which you have shown towards me for so many years. I have really thought of you constantly ; but the life which I lead during term-time makes it difficult for me to write letters."

In 1892 Bowen was still suffering from the troublesome consequences of his illness.

" I have had a bad time of it," he writes to Mr. Justice Mathew, in February of this year ; " Last week I certainly was much worse ; but I am once again going forward. The terrible weakness that I find the result of influenza, Butt, apparently, doesn't experience. But some people do ; and one begins to despair of ever getting off the sofa. In other respects I am progressing well enough. I mean to sit next term, *coute que coute.* Like Mrs. Chick, I think efforts must be made."

In the autumn of 1892 Charles Bowen and his wife passed some weeks at Braemar. His companions there observed with pleasure a marked improvement in his health and spirits.

"The shadow of his mortal illness," writes the
Warden of Merton, speaking of this period, "hung
over him long before its nature was acknowledged;
but I, for one, was deceived by the wonderful re-
cuperative power which he exhibited in 1892. During
August of that year I was staying at Braemar, to
which he came, partly by my advice, and where he
settled with Lady Bowen. . . . This was the last
time that I saw him at his best; and when I remarked
his buoyancy of spirits and vigour in walking over
the hills, I became quite reassured as to the soundness of his constitution. Judge Hughes and his wife,
together with other congenial friends, happened to
be there, and he was soon joined by his brother
Edward, who accompanied us on several mountain
excursions, amongst others in ascents of Lochnagar
and Ben M'Dhui, both of which involved several
hours' stiff climbing. Bowen declined riding on
Lochnagar, and dispensed with his pony for a great
part of the way on Ben M'Dhui. After my departure,
he made a second ascent of Ben M'Dhui, with other
long expeditions. On his return, he looked better
than I had seen him, but the effect did not last very
long."

Bowen returned to the South greatly
benefited by the sojourn at Braemar, but his
wife's health was now beginning to give him

great anxiety. Matters grew worse as the winter advanced, and for many months he was haunted by the dread of impending calamity.

In the spring of 1893 it fell to his lot to go upon Circuit, a duty which his wife's prolonged illness rendered especially burthensome. Those who were about him observed with pain the load which was weighing upon his spirits, and the serious effects of mental harassment upon a physique which at the best was barely equal to the calls upon it.

In August of this year Lord Hannen was compelled by failing health to retire from his duties as a Lord of Appeal, and Charles Bowen succeeded to his post. The appointment was heartily welcomed alike by the profession, the public, and the intimate personal circle, who hoped that the comparative lightness of the work might conduce to a restoration of his health, about which many were becoming increasingly anxious. "You need do nothing," said one of his friends, in enjoining this aspect of the case, "but assent to the judgments of your colleagues." "In that case," said Bowen, "I had better take the title of Lord Concurry." He had, unhappily, no opportunity of showing how impossible such a *rôle* would be to his ardent and conscientious nature. Shortly after his promotion, the Government requested Lord Bowen to undertake a piece of work which lay outside the regular scope of his new duties, but which he did not, on public grounds, feel justified in declining. This was to act on a Commission nominated by the Home Secretary for the purpose of inquiring into the circumstances of an unfortunate collision between a small body of soldiers and a mob at the Ackton Hall Colliery at Featherstone, the property of Lord Marsham, in Yorkshire. In the summer of 1893 the West Riding miners had gone out on strike, and at the close of July some eighty thousand had been thrown out of employment. In September, the concentration of the Police Force at Doncaster for the race week had left the county in an abnormally undefended condition in case of a breach of the peace. At the Ackton Hall Colliery a party of twenty-eight soldiers had found themselves confronted with a mob of some two thousand persons, who threatened to destroy the colliery works. The officer in command ordered a volley, and two persons were killed. The Committee—Lord Bowen, Sir A. K. Rollitt, and Mr. R. B. Haldane—were requested to inquire into the circumstances. The Report is of interest as containing a clear enunciation of the law—not previously free from obscurity—defining the duties of citizens, official and lay, civil and military—in giving aid against actual or apprehended violence at moments of public disturbance. For Lord Bowen's friends, the Report possesses a melancholy interest, for it was his last public work.

He was not, when he undertook the task, in a condition to justify that or any other intellectual or physical effort. He performed it—as every piece of work which fell to his lot—with punctilious care. His address on opening the Inquiry was observed as a type of dignified and self-contained eloquence. The Report itself bears the impress of thoroughness, research, and unwearying solicitude to deal with a grave question as its importance deserved. But it was the work of a man who knew that the close of his labours was near at hand.

His health had been declining throughout the year. In the autumn he went to Braemar, the air of which had done him so much good the previous year. But the result was disappointing. He made several walking-expeditions, and seemed for a while to be gaining strength; but the friends who were with him on both occasions could not but observe a marked deterioration of his bodily powers. He came back ill, and was met by the news that the Master of Balliol lay in a dying condition at Headly Park, the residence of his old pupil, Mr. Justice Wright. Thither Bowen hurried at once, and arrived just in time for an affectionate recognition during Jowett's last remaining hours of consciousness.

The last occasion on which Charles Bowen took an active part was one which I believe that, if he had had the choice, he would have chosen as the crowning act of his life. On December 2, 1893, a meeting was held in the theatre of the University of London, in Burlington Gardens, to consider the forms which could most appropriately be given to memorials to the late Master of Balliol. The Speaker presided. Lord Salisbury, as Chancellor of the University, moved the first resolution, expressing regret at the loss which the country and the University had sustained in the late Master's death. He was seconded by the Lord Chancellor and Mr. Asquith, who pronounced an eloquent and feeling eulogium upon Jowett's character and work. Lord Coleridge next moved a resolution to the effect that the Master's memory should be perpetuated, and his work carried on by raising a fund which might from time to time be applied to maintain, strengthen, and extend the educational work of Balliol College. He spoke with all the grace and charm of which he was so perfect a master, of his friend of fifty years—for he had become a Scholar of Balliol on the same day as Jowett became a Fellow—"of the loss which any fast and firm friend feels at the departure of another, and feels not the less because he knows that his own departure is at hand." Lord Bowen seconded the Chief Justice in a speech chiefly directed to explaining the form which it was proposed that the memorial should assume.

"I do not propose," he said, "to add to—by touching to tarnish—the tribute of affectionate and grateful words which have been offered this afternoon to the Master's memory by those in the State and in the University, who knew him. I desire only to add a few simple words by way of explanation, and, if justification be needed, of justification of the form which this Resolution has taken. This is a unique occasion. When great men pass away, the public retains a grateful sense of their services; and few

great men pass away, like the late Master of Balliol,
surrounded by an atmosphere of affection which
enabled him, at the close of an honoured life, to
count his friends, not, as some happy people can, by
scores, but by hundreds and thousands. For I will
venture to say that there is no part of the British
empire in which he had not friends and lovers, who
heard of his death with the deepest regret, almost
amounting to dismay.   This is a unique occasion,
because we have here amongst us a large body of
those who owe a debt which nothing can repay, and
no words describe, to the great College, the maintenance of which was the life work of the late Master.
Beyond and outside there is a larger and still more
important portion of the world, composed of men of
every opinion, of every shade of thought, political and
theological, who, differing as they must from the late
Master in many respects, are all united in this : that
there never has been given in our generation a nobler
type of a beautiful and devoted life.   To those of us
who were Balliol men, not much need be said in
favour of the Resolution which Lord Coleridge has
proposed.   Nothing that we can do for our ancient
mother, Balliol College, can wipe out the debt of
gratitude we owe her.   But of the larger portion of
the world outside who are interested in Balliol only
as one of the branches of a great University, perhaps
it is not too much to ask that they should trust us
with regard to this Resolution, as having been proposed

with the sole design of prospering the work to
which the late Master gave himself, and of selecting
that form of testimonial which would be most grateful
to himself, of which no better illustration can be
found than the perusal in the morning's papers of
the Will of the late Master, in which, after remem-
bering his friends and relations and dependents, he
devoted the whole residue of his modest fortune to
the advancement of learning in Balliol College. . . .
May I say that if the late Master can be touched at
all with knowledge of what is passing here, nothing
would give him a deeper sense of the affection and
sympathy of those friends and pupils and lovers
whom he has left behind than a proposal such as that
embodied in Lord Coleridge's resolution; that he
would feel that, in adopting it, we recognized and
understood the work which he has done, that the seed
which he had sown had fallen upon fertile soil, and
the labour of his long and devoted life had not been
in vain."

Those who heard Lord Bowen speak noticed
with sorrow his air of feebleness and distress.
It was his last public utterance and Lord Coleridge's.   In a few months both had followed
the friend whose loss was now their· common
sorrow, and whose merits their common theme.

Lord Bowen's health began rapidly to give way. Early in the following year, symptoms of the gravest order discovered themselves ; and, though it was still possible to question their full significance, it was scarcely more than a hope against hope that those who knew all could allow themselves to entertain. When the dreadful surmise became a certainty, there seemed still a chance—the last straw for love to catch at—that the progress of the malady might be retarded, and that some months of life might still be spared to him. Lord Bowen resolved that they could best be employed—for himself and for those to whom his life was dearer than it was, probably, to himself—by continuing, so long as it was physically possible, in the discharge of his public duties, and in the social intercourse which his many friendships brought naturally within his reach. For this it was, of course, necessary that his real condition, and its inevitable result, should not be known beyond the narrow circle who could be trusted

R

not to let the dreadful secret become public property.   It soon, however, became obvious that this programme—a sad one at the best—was not destined to be realized.   The disease made progress too rapid to allow of a hope for the shortest respite.   When it became certain that there was no room for hope, and that the end was near at hand, Bowen bowed with fortitude and submission to the overruling Will, and devoted himself to making the period of his suffering as little gloomy and painful as possible to those around him.   The bodily distress incidental to his illness was endured with unwavering serenity.   His cheerfulness remained to the last.   " In my life," said Sir W. Savory, who was consulted in the last illness, " I have never seen anything so touching as the courteous consideration which that dying man expresses in every word and gesture."

The news of the extreme gravity of Lord Bowen's illness, and of its near and certain

issue, came with a painful surprise to many of
the friends who, though they knew him to be
in bad health, had witnessed his recovery on
former occasions, and now were venturing to
hope that the vitality of his constitution might
carry him through another trial.   Only a few
weeks before his death did the terrible secret
escape, nor did it even then spread beyond a
very limited circle.   Mr. Gladstone, with whose
recently published translation of " Horace "
Charles Bowen's last hours of study had been
employed, wrote to Lord Rendel a letter of
warm sympathy.

"April 8, 1894.

" I cannot help troubling you with a line to say for
myself how deeply I feel for you all, and even, let me
add, how much more deeply I feel with you all, as to
the alarming illness of Lord Bowen and its probable,
though, I would fain hope, uncertain upshot.   I cannot help looking at such a man, with regard to the
interest which his country and his race have in him.
His great profession abounds with able and distinguished men.   But I am not sure that there was

ever one among them from whom so much was to be
hoped as from him, with reference to all those highest
interests of mankind which are at stake in the controversies and in the general movement of our unquiet,
though most deeply interesting, times. It so often
seems as if those were about to be taken early from
the world whom the world can least afford to lose.
But this is, after all, endeavouring to mend the
government of God, whose works and ways are so far
beyond our feeble grasp.

"I feel confident that he will look with a Christian
eye upon the prospect before him, and that the aid
will be found sufficient for him, which has been sufficient for so many that have preceded us, and on
which alone we that remain have to rely. Through
his great trial may the grace and power of God
effectually carry him to the land of rest.

"It would be a satisfaction to learn that his suffering was abated, and I trust that Lady Bowen bears
up, and is borne up, under the heavy trial."

Among the letters which Lord Bowen received at this time is one from Lord Coleridge,
which the friends of both men, each so close to
the end of his journey, will care to have preserved.

" March 4, 1894.

"MY DEAR CHARLIE,

"I do not at all like the message you sent me, though it was dear and good and like yourself to send it.   I shall not be back in London from Stafford, where I go on Tuesday, till the 13th or 14th, and then, if you see fit to see me, I shall make my way to you at once.   Meanwhile, though you do not need me to tell you, I am constantly thinking of you, and going back in thought to those days, when for years, we almost lived together, and when you were a friend such as I never had but one, and shall never have again.   I will not try to write out my heart.   You know it already.   God bless you, and give you back to those who love you.   My love to Lady Bowen.

"Always most affectionately yours,

"COLERIDGE."

During the early days of April, Charles Bowen's illness made rapid progress, and it became obvious that a few more days must bring the end.

Those for whom this memoir is compiled know far better than I the incidents of those last solemn hours: the sweetness and serenity

with which suffering was endured ; the consideration for others, which personal distress
seemed only to quicken ; the fortitude, and
resignation, and, to use his own almost dying
words, " profound humility" with which he met
his end.   To their recollections they may best
be left, unspoilt by any attempt to shape them
into words.   A few messages of affection to
some of his friends were the last that reached
the outer world.   On the morning of April
10th he passed away.

He was buried at Colwood, near the country
home where so much of his leisure had been
passed.   The spot is a lovely one.   The church-
yard commands a wide sweep of undulating
country, studded with the familiar objects of
a typical English landscape.   The sky was
flecked with the clouds and showers of early
spring as his friends gathered to his grave,
but presently the afternoon became lovely and
serene.   His son, and his old and faithful friend,
the Dean of Westminster, performed the last

office of friendship and religion.   As the
solemn rite proceeded, a skylark sprang into
the air, and, as if in unconscious derision
of human sorrow, poured out a flood of joyous
song, which still rang in our ears as we left
him to his long rest.   How much brightness
and sweetness seemed to many of us to have
vanished out of life !

At the same hour, another service was held
in Lincoln's Inn Chapel, where a great gathering of Charles Bowen's colleagues and friends
assembled to deplore their common loss.   One
of the officiating clergy was Lord Bowen's
much-esteemed friend, the Rev. William Rogers,
whose companionship at the Athenæum and
elsewhere had been among the pleasures of
later life.   He too has passed from amongst
us.   The Benchers of Lincoln's Inn resolved
on a permanent memorial, and an epitaph by
the polished pen of Mr. Justice Denman
perpetuates the testimony of Bowen's contemporaries.

In the vestibule of Lincoln's Inn Chapel a
marble tablet bears the following inscription :—

"IN MEMORIAM VIRI DILECTISSIMI
CAROLI SYNGE CHRISTOPHERI
BARONIS BOWEN DE COLWOOD
HUIVSCE HOSPITII NUPER E CONSILIIS
CUI ÆQUALES FERE OMNES
PUERO ADOLESCENTI ET ÆTATE FLORENTI
SE IPSOS POSTPONENDOS SENSERUNT
RUGBEIA QUOD ILLUM IN LUDIS ET IN STUDIIS
PRÆSTANTEM INSTITUERIT ADHUC GLORIATUR
OXONIA ILLUM COLLEGIUMQUE SUUM BALLIOLENSE
INTER ALUMNOS LECTISSIMOS COMMEMORANT
ILLUM OMNES JURISPRUDENTIUM ORDINES
COLLEGAM SOCIUM AMICUM
NON MAGIS ELOQUENTIA DOCTRINA SAPIENTIA
QUAM MODESTIA COMITATE ET SALIBUS
EXIMIUM AGNOVERUNT
NULLI QUAM NOBIS FLEBILIOR OCCIDIT
CRUDELI HEV MORBO ABREPTUS
A. D. IV. ID. APRIL
A. S. MDCCCXCIV
ÆTATIS SUÆ LX."

Rugbeians, old and present, did similar
honour to the memory of their school-fellow.
Oxford, a few weeks later, added a fitting note

of sorrow to the general lament over one of
the choicest of her sons.   At the Commemora-
tion in June of 1894, Dr. Merry, Rector of
Lincoln College, and Public Orator of the
University, discharging the traditional duty
of his office, mentioned, among other memorable
events of the year, his old college friend's
death in terms of graceful eulogy.

" Id quoque ægre ferimus, quod denuo Balliolensium
vicem dolere oporteat, quibus et Magistrum suum
deflere contigerit, et Visitatorem ; alterum plenum
annis ac laboribus pæne defunctum, alterum tem-
pestivam modo maturitatem assecutum, et summis
honoribus ac titulis nuperrime cumulatum.

"Venit mihi in mentem jucundissima CAROLI
BOWEN recordatio, quocum ego ipse studiorum com-
munitate et hilari sodalicio quondam fui conjunctus.
Quantam spem in optimo illo juvene collocavimus
cequales ;   quantum successum augarari, quanto
amore prosequi gaudebamus ! Lectissimo illi atque
ornatissimo adolescenti, omni lepore et venustate
affluenti, Musis amico doctrinæque studiis dedito,
nihil fere aliud denegaverat Natura nisi longum
vitæ spatium.   Dederat sane miram ingenii per-
spicaciam ; dederat facundiam, urbanitatem, elegan-

tiam, ita ut nemo fere in judiciis aut causas melius orare aut leges luculentius interpretari posset. His accedebat summa humanitas ac mores suavissimi ; nec verborum gratia decràt nec sermonis festivitas, seu scribendo vacaret, sive cum sodalibus colloqueretur. Dulcem animam avere atque valere jubemus."

To Lord Coleridge, the loss of Charles Bowen was a grievous personal sorrow.

"On the 20th of March," he writes to Sir M. E. Grant Duff, "Bowen borrowed a Horace of me, and spoke of a long sick-leave to get rest, and come back to his work really refreshed. I knew he had not a month to live, and that interview was hard work. You, dear old friend, immensely over-rate what I did for him. It was not a tenth, or a hundredth, part of what he did for me; but I did love him with my whole heart, and I thank God for the blessing of his friendship. . . . Jowett might have given an estimate of him, for no one has done so yet ; but he has gone first. How Bowen was loved, and how he deserved it !

> "Like clouds that rake the mountain summits,
>   Or waves that own no curbing hand,
>   How fast has brother followed brother
>   From sunshine to the sunless land ! "

One other expression of affection from Lord Coleridge, dictated during his last illness, and

signed with literally a dying hand, came to
Lady Bowen a few weeks after her husband's
death.   Lord Coleridge himself died a few
days later.

"Do not suppose, my dear Lady Bowen, that I
have forgotten or neglected your very kind letter;
it is useless to try to express what the loss of Charles
Bowen is to me.   I will not attempt it: I will only
say that it is a loss which I feel every day—if I said
every waking hour, I should not exaggerate the depth
of my feeling for him.   For four weeks I have been
hovering between life and death; they tell me now
that I shall recover, but if I do, I shall come back
into a poorer world, which never can be to me again
what it was a couple of months ago."

Here my task ends.   Would that the portrait were more worthy of its theme!   I have
tried to picture Charles Bowen's temperament
—sweet, joyous, affectionate; instinct with
natural gaiety, but crossed with sombre strains
of thought and a melancholy mood.   Conscious
of great powers, which a continued series of
successes forbade him to forget, and fired with
the ambition to play the part in life for which

he felt the capacity, he was haunted, throughout, with the misgivings which are the heritage
of thoughtful natures—misgivings as to the
scope and limitations of human existence, and
the real value of the prizes which life offers.
He was haunted, too, by sentiments and
motives alien to the sterner stuff of which
ambition should be made—delicate consideration for others—courtesy, the outcome of a
generous soul—nicety of moral judgment, a
fastidious taste. So it was that, in the struggles
and rivalries of professional life, he never made
an enemy, never provoked a grudge. So, too,
it was that in a wide circle of friends his death
was felt as one of the events which irreparably
dim the brightness of existence. It was, indeed,
to a "poorer world"—poorer in all that stirs
the soul to admiration and love,—that we returned the day we laid Charles Bowen in his
grave.

INDEX

Ainger, Rev. Canon, Master of the Temple, 192
"*Alabama* Claims," pamphlet on, 116
America, visit to, 225
Asquith, Rt. Hon., 148, 237
Athenæum Club, 200, 212
Austen Leigh, Rev. A., 42, 61-63 ; letter to, 95

Ballantine, Serjeant, 137
Bella, foundering of the, 135
Birrell, A., 191
Bowen, C. S. C., Lord, born 1835, 11 ; school at Lille, 13 ; at Blackheath, 16 ; at Rugby, 1850, 20 ; Parker Theological Prize, 1853, 23 ; Latin Essay and Queen's Medal for Modern History, 1853, 24 ; Balliol Scholarship, 24 ; Rugby Athletics, 27 ; Oxford, 1854, 32 ; Hertford Scholarship, 1855, 52 ; Ireland Scholarship, 1857, 52 ; Chancellor's Prize for Latin Verse, 54 ; Balliol Fellowship, 1857, 60 ; First Class, 1858, 61 ; Arnold Historical Prize, 1859, 64 ; Oxford amusements, 69 ; hard work at Oxford, 70 ;
letter to A. A. Leigh, 71, 81 ; from Goslar to A. A. Leigh, 87, 88 ; translations, "Sands of Dee," 77 ; "Crossing the Bar," 79 ; address to Birmingham Law Students' Society, 1884, 89 ; letter to Craig Sellar, 91 ; enters Mr. Christie's chambers, 93 ; travels in France and Italy, 95 ; called to the Bar, 1861, 95 ; engagement, 1861, first sessions, 98 ; joins the *Saturday Review*, 100 ; secedes from the *Saturday Review*, 102 ; marriage, 1862, 106 ; tour to the Riviera, 112 ; tour to Norway, 112 ; birth of eldest son, William, 1862 ; Maxwell, 1865, 116 ; Ethel, 1869 ; early times at the Bar, 129 ; appointed Junior Standing Counsel to the Treasury, 1872, 145 ; tour to Stockholm, St. Petersburg, Moscow, Kiev, Constantinople, 1878, 157 ; appointed a Judge, 1879, 157 ; declining health, 159 ; summer at Llantysilio, 1880, 160 ; letter to Hon. G. Brodrick, 161 ; purchases cottage at Slaugham Common, 1872, 151 ; settles at Colwood,

1881, 151 ; speech at Balliol, 1877, 153 ; appointed a Lord Justice of Appeal, 1888, 163 ; disinclination for legal authorship, 176 ; address to Birmingham Law Students' Society, historic method applied to Law, 1884, 177 ; essay in the *Law Quarterly* on the effect of recent Law Reforms, 181 ; essay in Mr. Humphrey Ward's Jubilee Volume on "Administration of the Law," 1887, 183 ; Committee of Council of Judges, 185 ; articles epitomizing its Report, 185 ; in Society, 187 ; the "Dilettanti" Club, the Athenæum, the Literary Society, "The Club," 188 ; elected Visitor of Balliol College, 227 ; Lord of Appeal, 233 ; death, 246

Bowen, Rev. Christopher, 11 ; curate of Woolaston, curate of Abbey Church, Bath, St. Thomas, Winchester, 12 ; death, 229

Bowen, Edward, 13, 16
——, William, 116
——, Maxwell, born, 1865, 116
——, William, born, 1862, 116
——, Ethel, born 1869, 132

Bradley, Dean, 20
Braemar, visit to, 231
Brodrick, Hon. George, Warden of Merton, 43
Bullock Hall, 42
Butler, Arthur G., 44, 56

Chamberlain, Right Hon. J., 131
City of London School, address to, 219
Classical Review, Professor Sellar in, 207
Cockburn, Chief Justice, 138
Cole, Rev. W. C., 43, 52, 57
Coleridge, Lord, 9, 192 ; letters from, 238, 245, 251

Colwood, burial at, 246
Congreve, Richard, 45
Conington, John, 44
Cook, J. Douglas, editor of the *Saturday Review*, 99
Cotton, Rev. G. E. L., 20
Cunynghame, H. H., Under-Secretary at the Home Office, 148

D'Alton, Count, 12
Davey, Lord, 44 ; estimate of Lord Bowen, 164
"Delphi" prize essay, 1858, 64
Denman, Hon. G., 191 ; epitaph by, 247
Dicey, A. V., 59, 61
Du Maurier, George, 191
Durham, Dean of, 40

Edinburgh Review, on "Essays and Reviews," 46
Ellis, Robinson, 20
Esher, Lord, estimate of Lord Bowen, 175
"Essays and Reviews," 46
"Essay Society," 56

Featherstone Riot Commission, 235
Fry, Lord Justice, estimate of Lord Bowen, 166

Gladstone, Right Hon. W. E., letter from, 243
Goschen, Right Hon. George J., 44
Goslar, life at, 85
Goulburn, Rev., 29
Grant, Sir Alexander, 43
Grant-Duff, Sir M. E., 48, 153, 185, 191
Graves, Miss Frances Steel, 124
Green, T. H., 20

Harcourt, Sir W. Vernon, 100
Hawkins, Hon. Mr. Justice, 138
Hereford, Bishop of, J. Percival, 61
Hermione, lines to, 214
"Historicus," 119
Holland, T. E., Chichele Professor of International Law, 61
Hope, Mr. A. J. Beresford, 100
Hughes, T., 123

James, Mr. H., 191
Jenkyns, Dr., 37
Jowett, tutor at Balliol, 9, 37; Commentary on Pauline Epistles, 38; attacks on, 39; essays and reviews, 46; letter to C. Bowen, on his marriage, 97; letter from, 123, 230; death of, 237; memorial meeting to, 237

Kenealy, 138

Lake, Dean of Durham, 40
Lecky, Mr. W. E. H., 191
Liddon, Canon, 191
Lincoln, Rector of, Merry, 42
Lincoln's Inn Chapel, memorial service at, 247; inscription on tablet in vestibule of, 248
London, life in, 1858, 89
Lyall, Sir A., 191

Mackonochie Case, the, 148
Mahaffy, Professor, on popular education, 220
Maine, Sir H., 100
Mark Pattison, 71
Master of Balliol, 9
Mathew, J. C., Hon. Mr. Justice, 138; letters to, 163, 197, 202; estimate of Lord Bowen, 171
Merry, 249
Merton, Warden of, 232

Nettlefold and Chamberlain, 131
Newman at Balliol, 41
Nightingale, Miss, 55
Norway, tour in, 113
Novel-reading, address on, 219

Oakley, John, Dean of Manchester, 59
Orator, Public, at Oxford, 249
"Old Mathew," a Wordsworthian parody, 143
Oxford, Reform movement at, 35; state of parties at, 35; Newman, J. H., 35
"Oxford Essays," 45

Palmer, Rev. Archdeacon E., 40
Pattison, M., 53
Pearson, Charles, 44
Percival, Rev. J., Bishop of Hereford, 61
Pollock, Chief Baron, 129

Rhoades, H. T., 21
Riddell, tutor at Balliol, 40
Royal Commission, reforms at Oxford, 47

Salisbury, Lord, 237
Sandars, T. C., 43
"Sebastopolis," Oxford Prize Poem, 55
Sellar, A. Craig, 42, 63; letter to, 91; death of, 227
——, Professor W. G., 207
Selwyn, Rev. E., 17
Smith, Henry J., 40
——, Goldwin, 100
Speaker, The, 237
Stanley, Arthur, Dean of Westminster, 101
Stanley of Alderley, Lady, 123
Steele, Lady, 12
Stephen, Sir J. F., 131, 191

Tait, Dr., 31, 32
Tichborne Case, 132
——, Sir John, 133
Totnes Bribery Commission, 131

Union Debating Society, Oxford,
　59; Bowen, President of, 60

Valescure, visit to, 229
Venables, George S., 100

Verses of the Wayside, 114, 213;
　Norway, 115
Virgil, "Eclogues" and "Æneid,"
　Translation of, 202

Walpole, Mr. Spencer, 191
Walsall Literary Society, Address
　to, 219
Wedgwood, Mrs., 132
Westminster, Dean of, 20, 191
Wodehouse, E., M.P. for Bath, 61
Working Men's College, Address
　to, 220

THE END.

PRINTED BY WILLIAM CLOWES AND SONS, LIMITED, LONDON AND BECCLES.

www.ingramcontent.com/pod-product-compliance
Lightning Source LLC
Chambersburg PA
CBHW031344020726

47499CB00005B/1389